Exotic D

Vol. III

By M.S. Parker

Copyright © 2015 Belmonte Publishing LLC

Published by Belmonte Publishing LLC.

ISBN-13: 978-1514177525

ISBN-10: 1514177528

Table of Contents

Chapter 1

Reed

I was aware that there were people around me, jostling to get in a better position to see their princess, but I barely heard or felt them. Every ounce of my attention was focused on her.

On the finger-shaped bruises on her arm.

It didn't feel real, like I was imagining things. Like my subconscious was making me see things that weren't really there, trying to convince me that Nami's marriage wasn't just one of obligation, but one of violence.

She was Princess Namisa Carrmoni, the next queen of Saja. She had fucking bodyguards whose entire purpose was to put themselves in harm's way for her. How the hell was her husband hurting her?

And I knew it had to be him. Tanek Nekane. The very thought of him made my already hot blood boil. I could picture the first time I'd seen him, sitting next to her, curling his hand around hers as if to tell me that she was his.

I couldn't just stand here and let her walk by, let her go back to *him*.

I didn't care that she had chosen him and that their marriage was none of my business. It didn't matter that we were on a public beach or that Nami was surrounded by bodyguards. I had to get to her.

I hadn't realized that I'd made the conscious decision to move until I was only a few feet away. I could see even more clearly how much she'd changed since the wedding. Her eyes, normally a warm, sparkling cyan, were dull and listless as they focused on the beach in front of her. Her skin was surprisingly pale under its normally golden shade. Pale except for the place on her arm where her make-up didn't quite cover-up the bruises. I doubted anyone else could see them unless they were looking closely, and even then, they didn't know her body the way I did.

I swallowed hard. She'd rejected me, married another man, but none of that changed how I felt about her. God help me, I loved her.

"Nami!" I called out her name as I took another step towards her, reaching out a hand.

I knew she heard me. I saw her body stiffen, her shoulders tense. She started to turn when one of the bodyguards said something sharply in their native language. I didn't get the chance to say anything else, to ask her to talk to me, because another bodyguard had decided he didn't like the American tourist being so friendly with his princess.

One large hand grabbed my arm, spinning me around so that I met the other hand as it was coming. The fist collided with the side of my face and pain exploded along my jaw. The blow made me spin around, tears welling up in my eyes. I shook my head to clear it, anger quickly overriding the pain.

I let myself complete the turn, let it give me extra momentum as I made a fist. He hadn't expected me to fight back so my punch caught him off guard. Still, he was solid and possibly military. A fist to the stomach didn't do more than make him double over for a moment before he rushed at me.

Maybe hitting him hadn't been my best idea.

Before he tackled me, I caught a glimpse of Nami's shocked expression before I landed on the hot sand. The bodyguard was shouting something, but it wasn't English so it didn't really matter. What did matter was keeping my arms up to cover my face and my knees up to my chest. I knew how to fight, in general at least, but I also knew how to protect myself when fighting back wasn't an option.

I heard Nami's voice, sharp and commanding. The man hitting me stopped and it didn't take a genius to figure out it was because of what she'd said. I waited for her to come over to me, but she didn't. I heard people talking, walking, but no one came near. After a moment, I opened my eyes. Nami was gone. A few people were staring at me, but there were no cops, no guards. Only my total embarrassment and the bruises I could feel already starting to form.

I winced as I straightened my legs and got to my feet. Sand stuck to my sweaty skin and my knuckles throbbed. I could feel the side of my face swelling. I needed to get out of here. I staggered back up to where I'd left my things, but left the beer in the sand. Someone would come along and claim it most likely. They were welcome to it. I'd had enough alcohol for today.

I made my way back to the hotel on foot. Air-conditioning and getting off my feet sounded good, but I preferred to get strange looks from people on the sidewalk rather than trying to explain my appearance to a cab driver. The desk clerk did a double-take as I came into the lobby. That, I supposed, proved more than anything else that while Saja did have its fair share of tourists taking advantage of the beautiful island, it wasn't a typical tourism kind of place. Somewhere like Las Vegas, they wouldn't have looked twice at someone stumbling in like me.

I made it up to my room without anyone else seeing me and headed straight for the bathroom. I scenario won out, they all ended the same way. With Nami dead.

No matter how hurt I was by her rejection, I still loved her, and even if I didn't, I wouldn't have wished that life on anyone.

Well, maybe on the abuser, I thought grimly. I wouldn't mind seeing Tanek getting a taste of his own medicine. I clenched my fist. I wouldn't mind giving it to him.

That wasn't what I needed to be thinking about though, I reminded myself. Tanek being punished had to be secondary to getting Nami out of that situation. I didn't know yet how I would do it, but I'd made the decision not to sit around and feel sorry for myself anymore.

I was going to save Nami. Even if she didn't want to be with me any longer, I would make sure no one ever hurt her again.

Chapter 2

Nami

I hadn't really noticed much of anything as the guards and I walked along the edge of the beach. I hadn't had any specific plans about where to go today. As part of mine and Tanek's honeymoon, we'd been expected to survey the country. We'd gone along the far side before circling back so that we were in the capital after only being gone for a week. I preferred this arrangement with my husband. He would be off doing his thing, leaving me to spend some time away from him.

Not that I could ever actually get away from him. The ring on my finger – Tanek's mother's – was the clearest visible reminder and I'd already perfected the art of not seeing it, despite its size. I was even able to push aside the weight of it. Not thinking about it should've been easy. The bruises were starting to fade and I barely felt anything from

Tanek's wedding night assault. I could almost pretend that the pain was from other types of exertion, hiking, walking, sight-seeing.

The people of Saja, however, wouldn't let me completely forget. They wanted to congratulate me on my marriage, offer advice. Some of the more superstitious ones offered blessings, sometimes accompanied by gifts of flowers and rocks – sorry, crystals – sometimes even potions. I wasn't entirely sure what to do with those until my mother told me that she had an entire closet full of these sorts of things. Reminders of a time gone by when magic was as real as anything else. Usually, I loved that Saja still retained that in some places, but now it was just one more reminder.

I was polite and smiled at each citizen, staying well-within the circle of bodyguards Tanek had insisted on me taking. New ones. I'd been grateful for them at first. I'd always had to be careful being out on my own, hoping that I wouldn't be recognized, but I hadn't realized how much higher my public profile would be after my marriage.

I'd assumed the new contingent of bodyguards had been to replace Tomas and Kai with ones I'd never met before. Ones who didn't have a direct personal connection to me. Tomas and Kai had never exactly crossed the line between employer and employee, but they'd kept my secrets, become my link to home when I'd been away. Moving them from being my personal guards to my sister's had been a smart move on Tanek's part. There wasn't anyone I trusted more to keep Halea safe. I just wasn't sure that even those two would be able to protect her from Tanek if I broke my word and turned him in.

I'd been thinking about all of these changes when we reached the beach. I wasn't sure why I'd decided I wanted to take a walk on the beach, only that I'd felt drawn here. Clean, fresh air. The tang of salt from the ocean. The breeze. It was beautiful, but I knew it wasn't the beauty that had put it in my mind.

As I walked along the waterline, I was forced to admit the little voice in the back of my head might have been right. I'd overheard a seemingly innocuous remark yesterday about an American who spent a lot of time on the beach, drinking beer. I had no real way of knowing if that American was Reed, but there weren't usually that many Americans on the island to begin with, and the woman's description had been of a tall, handsome man with golden hair and black eyes. I knew Reed's body well enough to build the image even without a more detailed description.

When I first started down the beach, I was sure it was just some sort of whim. A last ditch effort to catch a glimpse of the happiness I might've had. By the time I was halfway down the beach, I'd realized it had been a crazy idea. Seeing Reed again wasn't going to help anything, no matter how much I wanted it. Seeing him would only serve to remind me of what I'd given up and what I would never have.

A crowd was starting to form and I struggled to keep my chin up. It was surprising how quickly I'd learned to make myself invisible, hunching my shoulders, looking down. I couldn't let that carry over to my professional appearances. I had to appear as the same Princess Namisa that Saja had always known. Chin up, confident, ready to take on the world.

I didn't know how much longer I could keep up the facade. I was a strong person, but I could feel the wear already. It wasn't just physical, it was mental as well. Mental, emotional...every bit of me was exhausted. I didn't want to be out here. I used to love being around my people, talking to them, listening to their problems. Now, I felt the difference between us even more than usual. It wasn't just the extra bodyguards either. It was the way they circled around me, preventing anyone from even getting close or talking to me. I was apart. Different.

"Nami!"

I froze. None of my people would ever call me by that name. It was a personal name, a family name.

One that we used among ourselves or used as an alias. There was only one person I knew who would call me that name in that particular accent.

Reed.

The name pierced my heart. I wanted to grab onto the hope that sprung up, but I pushed it down instead. This had been a bad idea. I had no room for that sort of hope in my life right now. All I could truly hope for was survival and that my sister would be okay. The moment I'd allowed Tanek to put a ring on my finger, I'd given up the right to hope.

It didn't stop me from wanting to see him one last time, no matter how painful it would be. Even as I turned, I heard a scuffle and I watched as one of the new men tackled Reed to the ground. I opened my mouth to yell at him, to tell him to stop, but the words stuck in my throat. I watched in horror as my bodyguard hit Reed again, then kicked him.

Finally, I found my voice and called out a harsh command. After so many years of speaking primarily English, my native language felt strange in my mouth. I hadn't forgotten how to command though. They might have been hired by Tanek and were more loyal to him than to me, but there was still enough respect for the Saja monarchy that, unless it went against Tanek's wishes, my word was law.

The man beating Reed stopped, his face flushed,

15

breathing heavy. He looked annoyed at having been told to stop, but he didn't argue. Instead, he followed the rest of the men as they crowded back around me. They were closer this time than before, making me move at a faster pace until we were off the beach.

I went with them, resisting the nearly overwhelming urge to look back and see what had happened to Reed. It didn't matter that I still loved him. He wasn't my responsibility anymore. I couldn't think about his welfare. I had to think about my people, my family, my sister.

This past week had been like living in some sort of nightmare, one that didn't end when I woke up, but only began. Sometimes, I wasn't sure which was worse, the nightmares about losing Reed or waking up to the reality of what my life had become.

I'd hoped the honeymoon would give me the time to figure out a way to get Halea far enough away from Tanek to be safe. Once she was safe, I might be able to convince my parents of the truth. Instead, I'd been subject to public appearances where I had to pretend to love him, to be happy with my marriage. When I was worn out by them, we went back to whatever hotel we'd checked into for that day, and I'd be subject to Tanek's...affections. I'd stopped fighting him, but that hadn't meant he'd stopped hurting me. At least he'd refrained from hitting me as much.

16

And every night, before he fell asleep, he reminded me of what would happen if I dared to tell anyone about his treatment.

When we returned to the palace early, he cited an illness on my part, using the excuse to have me confined to my room for a couple days while he wormed his way even more deeply into my family. By the time I was deemed fit enough for a walk outside, Halea was only too excited to tell me just how much she'd been enjoying spending time with Tanek.

I should've had Halea on my mind as we made our way back to the palace. She should have always been the first thing on my mind, the only thing. I should have been thinking about how to get her away from Tanek, how to keep her safe.

The problem was, even with my eyes open, the only face I could see was Reed's.

Chapter 3

Reed

I didn't end up with a black eye, but the side of my face did turn some rather interesting colors. Fortunately, I'd spent enough time on the beach that I'd gotten a tan and the bruises weren't too obvious. My arms and legs were sore from where I'd blocked other hits, but overall, it wasn't too bad. The hangover was actually worse. Still, I refused to lay around in bed. I'd been moping for too long. I needed to get up and do something productive.

I spent most of Sunday trying to figure out the best way to approach the problem. I knew I had to do it from a logical standpoint rather than allowing my emotions to get involved. Whenever I thought of Nami being hurt, I couldn't think clearly. I wanted to go to the palace and demand to see Tanek, beat the shit out of him or challenge him to a duel or whatever it was people on Saja did when something like this happened. I considered lurking outside the palace until Tanek showed his face and then dragging him into an alley for a bit of turnabout.

As much as the idea appealed to me, I knew I couldn't do it. Not that I wasn't capable, but I knew that it would do more harm than good, not the least of which would be humiliating Nami. I couldn't do that to her, not on top of everything else. Plus, there was always the chance that she'd deny it all anyway and I'd end up in jail for assault. Tanek had to have something on her to have kept her from fighting back.

My next option would be to go to Nami's parents. I knew neither of them were very fond of me, but I also knew that they'd look poorly on anyone who risked tarnishing the family name. I had no doubt that Nami was hiding the truth from them as well.

The thing was, I didn't know which they'd consider the bigger scandal; that Tanek was beating their daughter or that someone was going to expose it. Parents who'd arrange a marriage to someone like that...I wasn't sure I trusted them to care more about Nami's well-being than they did about their good name.

I knew my own parents had cared more about the business part of my marriage to Britni than they had about whether or not I loved her, and that was bad enough. I liked to think that if I'd been in physical danger, my parents would've chosen me over business, but, in all honesty, I wasn't sure. If I was that uncertain about my own parents, I didn't think I could risk it with Nami's, especially when it would most likely be my word against Tanek's.

I needed proof. Evidence of some sort. I knew Nami. If she decided that she wasn't going to admit what was going on, she'd stick with it, no matter what. That meant she'd come up with some sort of excuse for any bruises. With her supporting whatever Tanek said, I'd get thrown out of the palace at the very least. Kai would make good on his threat at the worst. Instinctively, my hand went to my crotch. I had no doubt the bodyguard would indeed cut off my balls if he caught me talking to Nami again.

The first thing I had to do was discredit Tanek so that my own accusations would have more credence. That meant digging into his past. If I was lucky, I might even be able to find something bad. The problem was, I'd already proven that I was completely inept when it came to online research. This time, however, I couldn't involve any outside help. I had to do this on my own and discreetly.

That meant asking around.

Fortunately, I was able to play the ignorant American, fascinated with the whole concept of a monarchy. For the next few days, I made my way through various establishments, carefully asking about the new prince. I started at the hotel, asking members of the staff what they thought of Tanek. I didn't get much from them, but I hadn't really expected it. Employees at a place where discretion was certainly prized weren't likely to talk badly about members of the royal family. I had, however, seen the way several of the maids' eyes had flickered as they'd told me about the fairy tale life being lived by their princess. I hadn't been able to tell if it was jealousy or something more like worry.

The people of Saja were loyal, especially when it came to an outsider like me, but not all of them were skilled at keeping their feelings off their faces. By the middle of the week, I didn't have anything solid, but I did have a feeling that Tanek wasn't well-liked among most people. That, however, wouldn't be enough. Dislike of someone who'd been able to marry into the royal family could've easily been chalked up to jealousy. And even if it wasn't because he'd married Nami, Tanek's family was rich. I knew all too well how easy it was to hate people who'd been born into money. There'd been plenty of people in Philadelphia who'd hated my family just because we'd been wealthy. Well, I admitted, that might not have been the case with my entire family, especially my sister. Rebecca wasn't exactly a likable person.

she was here to try to trick me into something or she had something real. My gut said it was the latter.

"When I was seventeen, I went to work for the Nekane family as a maid," she began. She kept her chin up, eyes on me even though I could tell she wanted to look away while she told the story. "Tanek paid a lot of attention to me and I tried to discourage it. I told him I had a..." she struggled for the word "a suitor. That I was engaged. He did not care. It became so bad that I began to request a different schedule so that I was sure Tanek was out of the house, but that did not last long."

I had a bad feeling that I knew where this was going and it wasn't anywhere good.

"When I was nineteen, Tanek forced himself on me." The words were clipped, as if she had rehearsed them enough times that they no longer had any meaning, though the look in her eyes told me they hurt just as much now as they had the first time she'd said them. "I did not tell anyone the first time, or the second. Who would believe me?" The words were laced with bitterness. "He left shortly after the second time, going on a trip of some kind. I tried to find another place of employment before his return, but it soon became apparent that it would not matter."

She took a slow breath and reached into her pocket, pulling out a small rectangle. I took it as she spoke again. "I was pregnant."

The little girl in the picture looked to be about three years-old and she had dark hair like her mother. The eyes, however, were the same clear blue as Tanek's, though the girl's were warm.

"I went to his parents with the truth, telling them exactly what I told you, and they fired me, giving me two week's wages and a caution that I should never speak of this. When Tanek returned and discovered I was gone, he came to find me. He took me by the throat and pushed me against the wall. He told me that if I ever told anyone about what he had done or ever made claim that the child was his, he would kill me and our child."

A chill washed over me. I'd known Tanek was an abusive bastard, but I hadn't let myself imagine that it would be this bad. A sick feeling settled in my stomach as I wondered if he had forced Nami as well. I pushed the thought away. I couldn't dwell on it, not if I wanted to keep my composure.

"When I saw the announcement of his engagement to Princess Namisa, I considered going to the king and queen, but I was afraid," she confessed. "I would risk my own life, but not that of my daughter."

"Why come to me now?" I asked, surprised at how calm I sounded.

"I was at the beach," she said softly. "I saw the

princess and I knew that he was hurting her. And I saw you. When I heard that you were asking about Tanek, I knew you would fight for the princess."

I found myself nodding without conscious thought. "I will," I said. I stood and crossed the few feet between us before going down on my knees and taking Ina's hands in my own. "I will save the princess and I will make sure that Tanek can't hurt you or your daughter ever again."

It was a wild promise to make, I knew, but I wouldn't be able to live with myself if I got Nami away from Tanek and left Ina here to face his wrath. Whatever I did, I would make sure it made things safe for Ina and her daughter as well. I didn't love Ina, but it was the right thing to do, no matter how much harder it would make things. If I was going to be the man Nami deserved, it was the only thing I could do.

Chapter 4

Reed

As I made my way down the road that ran alongside the palace fence, I couldn't help but wonder if someone should tell the security guards about the ease with which a person could sneak onto the palace grounds. I'd gone in through the front door when I'd come to see the king and queen in the hopes that they could be convinced to allow Nami to choose her own husband. The first and last times I'd come in through a side entrance. The last time had been the day of Nami's wedding and I'd pretended to be one of the many people hired to work the event. No one had paid attention to me. The first time, I'd basically walked in through the gate, though not as bold. Somehow, I'd thought it should be more difficult to gain access to a royal family.

It was dusk as I approached the gate and I hoped that someone would be using the service entrance. The one thing I hadn't needed to do was climb over the wall and I didn't want to have to try it. I also didn't want to have to come back tomorrow. After what Ina had told me, it had been hard enough to not rush down here immediately. I'd needed to make preparations though. I couldn't just run in without a plan about what to do if Nami agreed to leave with me.

Not if, I told myself. When. She had to come. She couldn't just stay where she was and let Tanek beat on her until he finally went too far. As it was, I couldn't believe she hadn't left. I knew she had a sense of duty to her family and her country, but I never would have imagined that she would ever let a man hit her. If anything, I'd always thought she'd be the kind of woman who'd hit back. Then again, I'd never been able to imagine hitting a woman myself. Even Britni, at her worse, had never tempted me. Rebecca...well, we'd fought as kids, but that'd had nothing to do with her gender and everything to do with her being a bratty younger sibling. My gut told me, however, that something else was keeping her here.

I pushed aside thoughts of my family and everything else. I needed to pay attention. Getting caught trespassing wasn't the best way to get to Nami. In fact, it seemed like a pretty good way to get kicked off of the island, and I couldn't risk that.

As I got closer to the gate, I heard voices. I couldn't make out the words, or even if they were speaking English, but that didn't matter because I could hear the gate starting to creak open. A minute later, a man stepped out and I pressed myself into the ivy, praying it would hide me. He didn't even look in my direction as he turned and walked the opposite way. I didn't know if he was doing some sort of patrol or if he was leaving for the night, but it didn't matter. The door was starting to close and it was my only chance.

I darted around, muscles tense as I waited for a shout to signal I'd been spotted. Instead, the shadows of the falling night kept me from being noticed. I sidled along the inside of the wall, keeping my eyes on the guard standing by the small security booth. His back was to me as he studiously examined something on the ground, but even from a distance, I could tell that diligence wasn't high on his priority list. If this had been the only time I'd come through, I might've thought he was new or just bad at his job. As it was, I thought his behavior was about on par with everyone else's. From what I'd read of Saja's low crime rate, I supposed I shouldn't have been surprised.

I headed towards the door to the maid's quarters. The first time I'd been here, Nami had used it to sneak me into her bedroom. I didn't know if she'd since hired a personal maid or if Tanek would be in Nami's bed, but it was the best shot I had at finding her. If she wasn't there or if something kept me from getting inside that way, I would have to improvise and, while I'd enjoyed living for the moment when Nami and I had first met on the train, when it came to something like this, being spontaneous didn't seem like the best idea.

As I neared the door, however, I heard something. A low, sad sound that I instantly knew to be Nami crying. I wasn't sure how I knew it was her, only that the sound struck something inside me, pulling and twisting my guts. I abandoned my original plan to follow my instincts and immediately followed the wall to the left. Only a few feet away from where the building curved was a low garden wall. Even if it hadn't still been light enough for me to see glimpses of trees and flowers, the fragrance coming from behind the wall would've told me it was a garden.

The sound was coming from inside, so I made my way along the wall until I found an entrance and hurried inside. What little light I'd had was fading fast and the garden was shadowed. I could still make out a path and I kept to it until I found myself at a place where the path went to the right and Nami's cries came from the left. I stepped off the path and then realized that I was still on one, just one not well-worn. A few more steps and I found myself in a different part of the garden. The plants were wild here, made even more so in the waning light. I supposed it would've been quite beautiful in the daylight, but I only had eyes for the figure tucked behind what smelled like a rose bush.

"Nami?" I said her name softly, not wanting to startle her, but she jumped anyway. Her face was pale and I caught a glimmer of tears on her cheeks. Only now did I wonder how, if she'd been trying to hide, that she'd cried loud enough for me to hear her. I didn't take the time to try to figure it out though. It wasn't important.

I took a step towards her and she flinched. I stopped, pain and anger mixing with enough intensity to make my hands shake. "Nami," I said her name again, as gently as possible.

"Who's there?" Her voice was strong despite her tears.

"It's me." I shifted to the side so that the rising moon could at least give me a little light.

"Reed?" She pushed herself up onto her knees. She shook her head. "What are you doing here? You can't be here."

I closed the rest of the distance between us and crouched in front of her before she could move away. "I know and I've come to take you away."

"Know what?" The words were sharp.

I wanted to grab her, shake her, ask her how she could let someone hurt her like that, but I knew I wasn't truly angry with her. I was angry with myself for having let this happen. I should've seen Tanek for what he really was. I should've fought harder for her. I never should have let her send me away.

I swallowed all of those feelings. Blaming myself or wishing that I'd done things differently wouldn't change anything. "I know that Tanek is hurting you."

She stood up, anger flashing across her face. "Get out."

I stood as well, but didn't step back from her. "I saw the bruises on your arm at the beach. That's why I was trying to talk to you. I know you saw me."

"I saw you," she said. "And there was nothing for you to see. I'd been on the beach for hours. I had dirt smudges on my skin. That's what you saw."

"You don't love him," I kept going. "Why are you protecting him?"

She shook her head. "I'm not protecting him. You don't know what you're talking about. And I have accepted a marriage without love, not that it is any of your business."

"It is my business." The words came out more harshly than I'd intended. "I love you, Nami, and I'm not going to let him hurt you anymore."

She stared at me and I realized what I'd said. I'd

admitted it to myself, but I hadn't said it to her. I set my jaw, refusing to apologize or try to dismiss it.

"Reed..."

"I tried not to," I continued. "I told myself that you and I came from two totally different worlds and that it would never work. I tried to convince myself that it wasn't real, and when that didn't work, I told myself that if I truly loved you, I'd want you to be happy." I ran my hand through my hair. "I do want that, Nami. I want you to be happy, but I'll be damned if I didn't say that I want you to be happy with me."

"You can't love me." Her voice was small, broken.

I cupped her face in my hands and felt her entire body trembling. "I do," I said firmly. "I fought it because I didn't want to be in love, especially not with someone who I knew would only break my heart, but I couldn't fight fate." I wiped the tears from her cheeks. "We're meant to be."

Her face crumpled with a sob and I drew her against me. I didn't understand why she was crying, but she was in my arms, clinging to me rather than pushing me away, and I wouldn't fight her on it. She would speak when she was ready. It was dangerous for us to be here like this, but if she was going to leave with me, she had to come to terms with it.

After a few minutes passed, she began to talk

37

and I realized that it wasn't the idea of leaving the palace that had made her cry. Haltingly, she told me everything that had happened from the moment she'd told me to leave her bedroom. How Tanek had raped her, beaten her and threatened her sister. My arms tightened around her as I fought for control. I could feel the bile rising in my throat, threatening to choke me. I swallowed hard. If she could stomach telling me, I could stomach hearing it. One thing was for certain though. If I saw Tanek tonight, I wasn't sure I'd be able to keep from killing him.

When she finished, she looked up at me, face streaked with tears again. "I am so sorry."

"For what?" I smoothed her hair back from her face with one hand, my other arm still wrapped around her waist.

"I should have known...stopped him..."

I put my finger against her lips and the words died off. "No," I said. "None of what he did is your fault." I ran my thumb along her bottom lip. "If it's anyone's, it's mine. I should have fought harder for you."

She shook her head. "I told you to leave. I said that I'd made my choice."

"And I should have gone straight to your parents, told them how I felt and then beaten the shit out of Tanek for good measure." My voice darkened. "I should do all of that right now."

"No," Nami said. She reached up and put her hand on my cheek. "You can't do that."

"I know," I said reluctantly. "But I can do what I came here to do."

"Which is?" She was looking down now, as if she wasn't sure she wanted to hear what I was going to say.

I hooked my finger under her chin and tilted her head towards me. "Look at me," I said quietly. I waited until she did before answering her question. "I came to ask if you would leave with me."

Her eyes lit up and she raised herself on her toes, pressing her mouth against mine. I closed my eyes as my lips molded themselves to hers, pulling her body even more tightly to me until I could feel every line of her fitted along me. We were still in danger and there was so much more we needed to do, but for the moment, everything was right and I was going to enjoy it for as long as I could. Even if things went to hell when we opened our eyes, I had this to hold onto.

"Do you understand?" I asked, hearing the note of desperation in my voice. "I want to go with you, but I cannot leave Halea to the mercies of that man. I was willing to sacrifice my happiness to keep her from being miserable, but it's so far beyond that now."

"Go get her."

"What?"

"Your sister," he said. "I wouldn't leave any woman to Tanek, and certainly not your little sister. But I'm not leaving you here to take the abuse either. If your parents won't protect you both, then I will."

I wanted to argue with him that it wasn't a matter of my parents not caring enough to protect me. Instead, there was no way to guarantee Halea's safety while Tanek's case was decided. It would be my word against his and my parents already knew that I hadn't wanted to marry him to begin with. That was one of the things I feared, that they would see this as another aspect of me rebelling against what they wanted and by the time I could convince them of the truth, it would be too late.

"Hey." Reed squeezed my hand again. "I'm serious. Go get your sister and the three of us will get out of here."

"And go where?" I asked. "Do what? Halea's a minor. My parents could have you arrested for kidnapping."

He pulled me towards him and wrapped his arms around me, holding me so tightly that it almost hurt. "I don't care." He kissed the top of my head. "I have to do it."

"If you get arrested, it won't do us any good," I said as I leaned my head against his chest. I hadn't realized how much I'd missed the sound of his heart beating until I heard it again.

"I'll take you two someplace safe," he said. "And then I'll come back to talk to your parents."

I looked up at him, eyes wide. "You can't do that, Reed. If you go in and tell them that you took us..."

His near-black eyes were serious as he looked down at me. "I'm going to tell them everything, Nami."

I started to shake my head. "You don't understand..."

"If I'm willing to take the risk of telling them everything, then maybe they'll believe me when I tell them what Tanek's done." He twisted a curl around his finger. "It doesn't matter how much trouble I get in if it means Tanek's out of your life."

"Yes, it does," I insisted. "You can't risk it."

One corner of his mouth tipped up in a half-smile. "Nami, I'd risk anything for you. Without you..." He shook his head. "The only way I could live without you is if I knew you were safe."

I went on my toes again so I could brush my

mouth against his. I could see I wouldn't be able to talk him out of this. "What do we do now?" I asked.

He looked around. "Where's the safest place for me to wait while you go get Halea?"

I thought for a moment. "The maid's chambers. They're still empty."

He nodded. "All right. Get her and try not to be seen. We'll go out the service gate and then to my hotel. Tomorrow, we'll figure out the best way for me to approach your parents."

"They won't be here tomorrow," I remembered suddenly. "They left this morning on some diplomatic trip to Greece. They wanted me to go with them, but I told them I wasn't feeling well." My stomach twisted. "I didn't want to leave Halea alone here with Tanek."

Reed pressed his lips together in a flat line and I could see the anger in his eyes. I let it warm me, give me strength. He'd meant every word he'd said. He would fight for me, no matter the cost to him. I didn't want him to be hurt on my account, but now his protection extended to Halea as well. For her, I'd risk everything. Even the man I loved. And knowing he understood that made me love him even more.

"When will they be back?" Reed asked.

"Wednesday night," I said. The thought of having to stay here with Tanek until then made me sick.

Reed nodded, but didn't say anything. His arms were still around me, but I could see his expression was far away. I didn't ask any questions, giving him the time to think things through while I allowed myself to relax in his embrace.

"We do this tonight," Reed said finally. "We'll still go back to my hotel room. Tomorrow morning, I'll make arrangements to get us out of the country."

"As soon as Tanek realizes we're gone, he'll be looking. He'll check the airport."

"Then I guess we'll have to rent a private plane to take us somewhere in Europe and we can decide where we want to go from there."

I started to shake my head. "He'll be monitoring my bank accounts and credit cards."

"Who said you were paying for any of it?" Reed gave me a small smile. "I may not be a prince, but I can take care of my princess." He kissed my forehead and then released me. "Let's go. The longer we wait, the more dangerous it becomes."

He was right and I reached out to take his hand as I led him out of the garden. We went back the way he came. Besides being quicker than going the other way, it also meant I didn't have to walk past the place where Tanek had attacked me. I moved cautiously, keeping an eye out for the new guards Tanek had assigned to me, but they weren't anywhere around. Over the last few days, as long as I was in the palace, Tanek hadn't insisted I be followed. He'd known I'd never leave as long as Halea was in danger.

Reed slipped into the maid's chambers and I gave his hand a quick squeeze before leaving him. My insides twisted as I walked away, but I reminded myself that this time was different. I was coming back and then we'd leave together. I wouldn't lose him again.

Chapter 6

Reed

Waiting for Nami to come back with Halea was one of the hardest things I'd ever had to do. Now that I knew the full extent of Tanek's abuse, every moment of Nami being gone was agony.

Scenarios kept running over in my mind. Everything from Tanek beating her until she gave me up to Tanek hurting Halea because of me convincing Nami to run. I kept seeing her face, bloodied and bruised, her body being used...

I shook my head and began to pace. The main room wasn't very large so I counted off steps to further distract me. If I didn't concentrate on something else, I would go after her and damn the consequences. The only thing that kept me from doing just that was the knowledge that if I did, I'd be putting both Nami and Halea in even more danger. If Tanek caught the two of them together, most likely he'd just guard them more closely. His control over Nami only lasted as long as her sister was safe. If he hurt Halea for small infractions, his secret would be harder to hide and from what I'd learned, Tanek hadn't gone this far without being arrested by making stupid decisions. He was cruel, but calculatingly so.

I was starting to imagine all of the various ways I wanted to hurt him when the door to Nami's bedroom opened. I froze. Just because I was expecting it to be Nami didn't mean it would be. A moment later, I let out the breath I was holding. Nami smiled at me as she came into the darkened room. Behind her was a young woman who looked so much like Nami's mother that I could see what the queen had looked like as a teenager.

"Halea," Nami said softly. "This is Reed Stirling. He's going to get us out of here."

Halea's face was pale, but I could see the same steel in her that I'd seen in Nami. The girl held out her hand. "Nice to meet you."

I shook her hand and then turned to Nami. "Did anyone see you?"

"No," she said. "Not as far as I know." She glanced at her watch. "But we need to go before someone realizes we're missing." She walked past me towards the outside door. "I'll go first."

I opened my mouth to protest, but she gave me

one of those looks that I knew she'd use when on official business.

"I'll check to see if anyone's out there. There'll be questions, but I'm not a stranger," she said. "Halea follows me and you come behind her to make sure she's safe."

I glanced at Halea, wondering just how much Nami had told her sister about why we were sneaking away. Judging by the stubborn set to Halea's jaw, it had been enough to convince her. I just hoped Nami had spared Halea the details. I couldn't imagine how guilty she'd feel if she knew Nami had stayed with Tanek to protect her.

Nami opened the door slowly and peered out through the crack. After a moment, she opened it wider and stepped outside. A few seconds ticked by and she motioned for us to follow. We stuck to the shadows as we went, but most of the guards seemed to be centered around the front of the palace. A few were patrolling along the fence, but they were easily avoided. When we reached the gate, however, we encountered a different problem.

The gate was closed. Before, I'd just waited until someone had needed to use it before sneaking in. That wasn't an option right now though. There were three of us and, any moment, someone could realize that the girls were gone.

We needed another option.

"I'll get him out of the booth," I said softly. "You two open the gate and get out. I'll follow as soon as I can."

To my surprise, Nami rolled her eyes. The gesture seemed so casual, especially considering our present circumstances, that it almost made me laugh.

"I thought we might need a distraction," she said. She held up a hand-held radio.

There was a hint of a smile on her lips and I felt a wave of relief go through me. I'd been worried that I would lose her to what had happened, but now I could see that she was still in there. We could get through this.

She pressed down on the button and said something in her native language. I caught 'Namisa' and that was about it. Before I could ask her, Halea spoke in a soft voice, her English as perfect as her sister's, though her accent was thicker. Nami had spent a few years in America recently.

"She asked for the name of the guard at the security booth and then told him that she did not receive a package she was expecting. She is telling him now to go look at the end of the street to see if it was left there."

"Thanks," I whispered. I gave her what I hoped was a reassuring smile.

This had to be completely disconcerting for the

poor girl. One minute, her life is fairly normal, and the next, she finds out that her sister's being abused and they have to leave with someone she doesn't know, going somewhere unknown.

I didn't have much more time for speculation as I heard the gate creak open. The security guard in the booth was walking towards it. Nami held up her hand, cautioning us to wait. It was funny. I'd thought I was coming to rescue her and now she was the one responsible for actually getting us off the grounds. Then she glanced back at me and I saw the fear in her eyes. She was absolutely petrified that this wouldn't work, and I didn't need her to tell me to know that the only thing keeping her together was Halea.

Nami took a few steps out of the shadows and looked around before gesturing for us to follow. Halea and I followed Nami over to the gate and then out. Instead of turning towards the street, however, Nami turned the other way. As we went, I remembered Halea saying that Nami had sent the guard to the street to look for her non-existent package. Smart.

Nami led us down another side-street and then back up to the street that ran in front of the palace. As soon as we reached it, she stopped and turned to me.

"Where to now?"

Her voice was strong, but I could see the weight of it all in her eyes. I reached out and took her hand. I wanted to take her in my arms and kiss her, tell her everything would be okay. I couldn't do that with her sister here, not without making Halea either embarrassed or nervous. I didn't know how much Nami had told her about me, after all. Instead, I settled for squeezing her hand and letting her see on my face that I was taking over. She didn't have to be strong anymore. I saw the relief on her face, but she hid it quickly. She would still be strong as long as Halea could see her.

"We're going back to my hotel," I said. "This way."

I hated the idea of making the women walk, especially since both of them were wearing shoes that were more conducive for walking around a palace rather than walking down the sidewalk, but Saja was a small country and their royal family well-known. No one on the island would not recognize either princess. We couldn't take that risk. At least walking, they could keep to the shadows.

When we arrived at the hotel, I put myself between the desk clerk and the women, advising them to turn their faces away as we came in. I supposed the clerk would think I was bringing prostitutes back to my room, but as long as he didn't realize who Nami and Halea were, I was fine with

56

that. My reputation wasn't exactly foremost on my mind at the moment.

Halea's and Nami's reputations, however, were my concern.

"Bathroom's right there." I pointed. "Bedroom's through that door. You two can share it. I have some clothes in there you can use until tomorrow."

Halea and Nami exchanged one of those sibling looks. I didn't know what they communicated in their silence, but after a minute, without a word, Halea walked into the bathroom.

As soon as the door closed, Nami turned to me. I took one step towards her, my arms open, and she fell into them.

"Thank you." The words were muffled as she buried her face against my chest. I felt the tension flow out of her body and she sagged against me. "Thank you for saving her. For saving me."

"Always," I promised.

I wanted nothing more than to keep her in my arms, take her into the bedroom and make love to her until every bad memory was banished from her mind. But I knew it wasn't only Halea keeping me from doing that. I loved Nami and I wanted her, but I would let her initiate all physical contact. I would do whatever it took to make her feel safe again.

"Sleep tonight, my love." I smoothed down her curls. "You're safe here."

I had Nami bring me out a pair of shorts and waited until the sisters were in the bedroom with the door closed before I went into the bathroom and changed. I left the light on and the door cracked so that if either one needed to use the bathroom in the middle of the night, they would be able to see that I was still asleep on the couch.

I wasn't sure when I'd ended up falling asleep, but the soft shuffle of feet on carpet woke me some time later. I looked up to see Nami standing at the end of the couch. I sat up, immediately looking around for the threat.

"What's wrong?" I pitched my voice low, not wanting to alarm Halea if she wasn't already awake.

Nami walked around to the side of the couch and I could see now that she was wearing one of my t-shirts. It hung down to mid-thigh, nearly as long as some dresses I'd seen. My stomach tightened as I wondered what she was wearing underneath. I immediately pushed the thought away before my body could respond even more than it already was.

"Nami." I started to sit up, but she shook her head. "What...?"

Whatever question I'd intended to ask was lost as Nami pulled my blanket off and dropped it on the floor. I swore softly as she straddled my waist, her hand hot on my stomach as she steadied herself.

"You don't have to..." I groaned as she grasped

my cock through my shorts.

"Please." Her voice was soft. "I need to remember that it can be good."

My heart twisted at her words and I felt a surge of hate for Tanek, for what he'd done to the woman I loved.

Suddenly, she moved her hand and turned her face away. "I understand," she said, her voice empty. "I am not..."

I sat up so quickly she gasped, losing the rest of her sentence.

"Don't." The word came out harsher than I'd intended and even in the low light, I saw her flinch and hated myself for it. I softened my voice and cupped her face as gently as I could. "I want you so badly," I confessed. "But I don't want to hurt you."

She let her weight settle more firmly on my lap and I knew she could feel my cock hardening against her ass. Her eyes locked with mine and she slid her hand across my chest. I put my hands on her hips, fighting the urge to take control. I'd told her the truth, but mere words weren't enough to convey the depth of what I felt for her.

"I need you inside me." Her nails scraped across my nipples and I hissed. "Do you need...?"

She didn't need to finish the sentence. I knew what she wanted. I wanted it too. I shook my head. "What about...?"

59

Her face hardened for a moment. "The one thing I can say is that even if he has been with others, he would not dare risk the health of a possible child. He's healthy and has been faithful." The last word held more venom than I'd realized she could possess.

I reached up to run my fingers down along Nami's cheek. "Are you sure? I would never ask you to do something you don't want."

She flexed her hand, digging her nails into my chest. "I want."

There was a ferocity in those two words that sent blood rushing to my cock so fast that it almost hurt. She leaned forward and our mouths crashed together hard enough to bruise. She pushed her tongue between my lips and my hands bunched the fabric of my t-shirt. I wanted to feel her skin so badly that my hands were shaking.

I broke the kiss, my chest tight. "I need to know..."

She froze in my arms.

"I need you to tell me what to do." I kissed her jaw and she relaxed. I looked at her and realized what she'd thought I was going to ask. "I will never ask you to re-live any of that," I said, tucking a curl behind her ear. "I'll be an ear if you need one, but will never ask."

She nodded.

"Now." I kissed the corner of her mouth. "Tell me how you want me."

"On top."

My eyebrows went up at that. I'd thought for sure she would want to be in control. Not that I would complain. I didn't care how she wanted me, only that she did. "Are you sure?"

She nodded.

I wrapped my arm around her waist and managed to turn us over without either one of us falling off the couch. As I settled between her legs, I slid one hand up over her thigh and hip, venturing under the t-shirt to answer my previous unspoken question. My hand found nothing but skin beneath the cotton.

Nami's hands pushed at the waistband of my shorts and I could feel the shift in the air between us. There was an urgency now that hadn't been there before. An edge of desperation to the need that we both had.

"Inside me." Nami's breath was hot against my ear. Her hand slid around my hip and wrapped around my cock. "Now."

I covered her breast with my hand even as I surged forward, burying myself inside her. Her back arched and I saw her bite her bottom lip to muffle her cry. My entire body shook with the effort to stay quiet. I rested my forehead against hers for a moment, struggling for control.

"I love you," I whispered. My hand tightened around her breast.

"Then love me." She rested her heels against the back of my knees.

This wasn't the tender, gentle love-making I'd imagined she would want. This was something deeper and our bodies moved against each other with an almost primal need. My fingers moved beneath her t-shirt, rolling and tugging on her nipple as soft, whimpering sounds fell from her lips, mingling with my own harsh breathing.

It wasn't long before she began to gasp and moan, the sounds of pleasure that I'd been dreaming about. I could feel my own climax coming and fought it, determined to feel her come around me before I let go. I leaned down and pressed my face against her neck. As I nipped at her throat, her nails dug into my shoulders and we came together, her pussy tightening around my cock as it pulsed inside her.

"Thank you," she whispered.

I could feel hot tears against my skin as Nami held me to her. I hated the circumstances that had brought us back together, hated what had happened, but I loved having her back in my arms. For her, I'd thought I'd left behind my home, but I knew now that wasn't the case. She was my home.

Chapter 7

Reed

I was deep in the best sleep I'd had in weeks when a loud bang jerked me out of it. For a brief moment, I couldn't remember where I was or what was going on, but then I saw the men coming into the room and immediately reacted.

I rolled off of the couch, hearing Nami make a noise but not looking at her. She was safe at the moment and I had to keep her that way. I needed to get between her and the men. I barely even registered the fact that I was naked.

It was only after a few seconds that I realized the men were cops and they had guns pointed at me. I automatically put my hands up, but I didn't move from my place in front of Nami.

I heard her suck in a breath as Tanek came into the room and it was only knowing that I was shielding her that kept me from going after him.

"Down on your knees!" one of the cops shouted.

"Not until he leaves." I jerked my chin at Tanek. "You get him out of here, keep him away and then I'll get on my knees."

I wasn't sure where things would've gone from there because the bedroom door opened and Halea stepped into the room. Before I could move or speak, Tanek was there, grabbing Halea and pulling her towards him.

As soon as I heard him speak, I knew what he'd done.

"Please tell me he did not harm you as well, dearest."

My jaw dropped, my attention caught for a split second, just long enough for the cops to move. As I was thrown to the ground, my arms yanked behind my back, I managed to get out a question. "What are the charges?"

"Kidnapping." The cop jerked on my wrist and a sharp pain shot up my arm.

"And rape."

Tanek's voice cut through the chaos and I heard Nami gasp at his words.

"I am so sorry, my darling," Tanek continued. "That I did not arrive in time to stop him."

One of Tanek's personal guards came into the room and Tanek pushed Haley toward him. "Bring this innocent child to the car and wait for us. She

such as kidnapping, rape and murder were always tried in front of the king and queen. They couldn't recuse themselves. They would have to hear every detail, whether real or made up.

I watched, helpless, as they dragged Reed from the room.

"We must take the princess to the hospital. She need to be examined by a doctor." The police officer speaking with Tanek was slightly older than my husband, but it was clear the man was out of his depth.

"No," Tanek said firmly. "If the princesses go to the hospital, someone will talk. We need to keep this quiet."

I could feel his eyes on me.

"Princess Namisa is my wife and I would not have her dishonored this way."

I ground my teeth together and prayed for the self-control I needed not to rush at Tanek and attack him. With Haley in the hands of Tanek's guard I couldn't do anything, for now at least.

"What do you wish us to do, Prince Tanek?" the officer asked.

"You may secure this as a crime scene regarding the charge of kidnapping. Let people think it was for money."

I almost laughed at that. I hadn't looked into Reed's family, but I knew they were wealthy. All he had to do was hire a good lawyer who'd submit his bank statements and it would be clear that Reed wasn't after money. Then I remembered what he'd said about having given up much to be with me. If that had included his family's fortune, Tanek might be able to sell the kidnapping charge.

"I will take the princesses back to the palace," Tanek continued. "From there, I will summon a discreet physician who can examine my wife."

I risked a glance now. Tanek wasn't looking at me. The cop, however, was. He looked nervous and I didn't blame him. It was clear that he wasn't entirely sure what to do. He knew protocol and he wanted to protect his princess. He just wasn't sure how. I gave him a slight nod and saw the relief in his eyes.

"Very well, Prince Tanek."

"And, Officer?" Tanek spoke as the cop was about to walk away. "Make sure your men know not to breathe a word of the secondary charge. I am sure the king and queen wouldn't look too kindly on those who disparaged their daughter's reputation."

"Yes, Sir."

I felt a faint stab of vindictive joy at the anger on Tanek's face at not being referred to as 'your Majesty'. It was bad enough that he could demand to be called Prince. As heir to the throne, I was referred to with the same honor as both of my parents. Tanek would be unable to demand that title until I became queen.

And I didn't intend for him to be at my side when that happened.

"Princess Namisa." Tanek turned to me, eyes still flashing at what he considered to be an insult. "You should get dressed before we leave."

I nodded and hurried into the room and grabbed the clothes I'd been wearing yesterday. After a moment's hesitation, I took a t-shirt from Reed's bag and pulled it on over the camisole I'd been wearing. I could claim modesty and Tanek wouldn't argue, not in front of anyone. I closed my eyes and allowed myself a moment to feel the soft cotton on my skin, to breath in Reed's scent. It calmed me, and I opened my eyes.

When I walked out into the room, I kept my shoulders hunched, my arms crossed against my stomach. For all intents and purposes, I was the victim. As long as I played my part, my sister was safe. Tanek would know that it wasn't real, especially when he realized I was wearing one of Reed's shirts, but that didn't matter.

"Are you ready to go home?" Tanek made his question seem friendly, concerned, but I knew the truth.

"Yes." I allowed him to take my arm, stifling a wince as he dug his fingers into my flesh.

The police officers all bowed their heads as I

71

walked past and I knew it wasn't only a sign of respect, but an acknowledgement of what they thought had happened to me. I kept my eyes straight ahead as we came out into the hallway. The hotel wasn't very full, but what few guests they had on this floor were in the hall, wanting to know what was going on. I could feel their eyes on me, hear whispered rumors. As we reached the elevators, Tanek shifted, putting his arm around me instead. I guessed he wanted the gesture to look comforting, but he still managed to situate himself so that his fingers could pinch my waist.

Outside the hotel, I was relieved to see no reporters, only a car. The driver opened the door and Halea was there. She looked concerned but thankfully, unhurt. No matter what happened to me, I was determined to protect my sister. As we settled in the car, Tanek pulled me close, sliding his hand under the t-shirt and grabbing my breast. I made a small pained sound as his grip tightened and that seemed to satisfy him for the moment because he didn't make it worse.

He pressed his mouth against my ear, pitching his voice low so that Halea couldn't hear him. "You will pay for what you did."

My stomach flipped and I twisted my fingers together to keep my hands from shaking.

"Your parents are gone until Wednesday. They

do not know anything about what happened, so they will not be coming home early to rescue you from your punishment."

I pressed my lips into a flat line, refusing to give him the satisfaction of another sound.

"Every night from now until they return, I will beat you until you learn your place. If my fists cannot convince you, then perhaps I will borrow a whip from the stables." His fingers grasped my nipple, twisting it painfully. "Once I have finished with that part of your lesson, I will use you in whatever way I please." He switched from our native language to English. "Your mouth. Your cunt. Your ass. You are mine. You will bear my son and he will make this country great."

I had no doubt that he meant it all, or that once I gave him a son – I knew he wouldn't be satisfied with a mere daughter – my life would no longer have any importance. What I feared was that he would become impatient if pregnancy proved as difficult for me as it had been for my grandmothers and my mother. Would he simply get rid of me and take Halea? It wasn't something likely to happen soon, but I had a feeling that he wouldn't wait very long, probably only until Halea turned eighteen.

All of our guards came to greet the car and I wondered how Tanek's men had explained the escape. I was actually surprised to see them all there rather than in jail or beaten to a pulp. Tanek couldn't have been happy when he'd discovered Halea and I were missing.

"Kai, Tomas, take Princess Halea to her room."

Both men glanced at me as they gestured for Halea to come with them. I avoided meeting their eyes. They couldn't know what Tanek had done to me. They would either kill him or go to my parents. While the first would relieve me of my problem, it would also put them in prison, no matter what their reasons had been. The second would put Halea in more danger.

"Claudel."

A tall guard of French descent stepped forward. He was a grim-looking man, the kind that would've looked more at home lurking in a dark alley than he did here.

"Escort Princess Namisa to our chambers."

Claudel gave Tanek a sharp nod.

"Keep the princesses in their rooms. Lock them in if necessary. They are not to leave."

What was Tanek doing, I wondered. Was he going to lock me in my room for hours, letting me imagine all the things he planned to do to me?

He switched to English as he answered my unasked question. "I will be going to the police station to deal with the criminal who dared kidnap our princesses." He glared at his guards. "And I will expect, upon my return, a competent explanation of how this happened, who is to blame and what is being done to prevent it from happening again." He threw a glance in my direction before returning to the guards. "Punishments will be dealt out when I return."

He got back into the car and Claudel came over to me.

"Princess," he said stiffly as he offered me his arm.

He wouldn't be violent if I refused, I knew, but I also knew that word would get back to Tanek and this small act of rebellion didn't quite seem worth the price I knew I would pay.

I took his arm and let him lead me into the palace and through the corridors to the room I shared with my husband. As the doors shut behind me, I sank to the floor and wrapped my arms around my knees.

What had I done?

I rested my forehead on my knees. "Reed," I whispered. "I am so sorry." Hot tears slid down my cheeks. "I'm sorry."

least of a sexual encounter. I was actually surprised they hadn't taken me straight to a doctor to get swabs and take pictures and all that.

Fuck. I ran my hands through my hair. Was that what they were doing to Nami right now? Forcing her to get a rape kit done?

"Oh, baby, I'm so sorry," I whispered.

I'd never thought she'd have to be subjected to this sort of humiliation. It was only now that I wondered if I'd left marks on her. Had I bitten her? I knew I hadn't been gentle. She hadn't wanted me to be. And now, even if she was able to feel safe enough to say that the sex had been consensual, people would know some of her preferences. That sort of thing was awful enough for someone not in the public eye, but for a princess...I could only imagine what she was going through.

I closed my eyes, my head resting in my hands. What was I going to do? I wasn't too worried about myself. I had the money to hire a good lawyer and the connections back in the States to put some pressure on Saja if I needed to. But Nami and Halea, what was I going to do about them?

"Piece of shit American."

I looked up even though I didn't need to see him to know Tanek was the owner of the voice. He stood on the other side of the cell door, a smug look on his face. I stayed where I was, not trusting myself not to do something stupid...like smash his face against the bars repeatedly until he was unconscious.

"Did you know that, in Saja, kidnapping can be considered a capital crime? If royalty is involved, the death penalty is almost always added to the charge." His pale eyes glittered, giving me a glimpse of what Nami faced every day. "Add rape onto that and I believe that an execution will not only be requested, but required."

I fought to keep my voice calm. "Threatening an American with the death penalty, particularly for actions that you know to be false, sounds like a good way to start an international incident."

Tanek shrugged. "The United States has executed plenty of people who are innocent." His eyes narrowed. "And we both know I have evidence that can be used to prove your guilt."

I slowly stood up, keeping my eyes locked on his face. I knew his type. He was the kind of man who took pleasure in bullying people, trying to prove that he was a man by pushing around whoever he could. I might be the one in jail, but I wasn't about to let him think he could bully me.

I kept my voice even, but didn't bother to try to hide my anger and disgust. "What we both know, Tanek Nekane, is that, of the two of us, only one is guilty of rape."

His face twisted and he snapped something over

his shoulder in Saja's native language. It didn't sound nearly as beautiful as when Nami spoke it. Then the door slid open and he was coming inside.

I knew what would happen and that I had only seconds to make a choice. I could fight back, probably get in a few good blows before someone came in. But even if he started it, I was the one who'd be charged with assault and, unlike the other two charges, I would be guilty of this one. I wasn't sure what the penalty would be for assaulting a prince, even one who married in, but I was sure it wouldn't be good for me.

That left me with the alternative. Take it.

He wouldn't kill me. At least, I didn't think he would. A trial and a death sentence would be bad enough. If he beat me to death while I was in police custody, even being the prince wouldn't protect him. A small part of me had the fleeting thought that if that happened, at least Halea and Nami would be safe.

And then he was there and I realized I'd already made my decision. I turned as he swung and his first hit caught me in the shoulder. I might not fight back, but that didn't mean I was going to stand there like an idiot. I kept my hands up, palms out. Tanek was angry, but he didn't fight stupid. Considering how well he'd been able to hide his actions, I had expected nothing less. I managed to block and dodge two more swings, but the third one caught me in the temple.

Stars burst in front of my eyes and I staggered back. Tanek hit me again, this time in the stomach and all the air rushed out of my lungs. A kick to my leg put a knot in my calf and I went down on my knees. I saw where the next kick was aimed and twisted so that it caught my hip. Pain flared through the muscle and I curled up, protecting my head and stomach as Tanek kicked and hit me. My ears were ringing, head swimming, and then I realized I wasn't being hit anymore. I risked a glance up and saw one of the cops pulling Tanek back out of the cell. I waited until the door closed before I uncurled, wincing at the pain. I'd barely healed from the last beating I'd gotten and Tanek had managed to catch a couple of the still tender spots.

The pair were speaking in their language, but based on the way the cop was glaring at me, I had a feeling that whatever Tanek was saying wasn't very complimentary. I tasted blood on my lip and could feel it swelling. Damn. Anger flared as I thought of him going after Nami like that and I stood, ignoring the pain.

"Tanek." I spit some blood into the sink. "I gave you that. Next time, you'll find out what it means to pick on someone your own size."

Tanek glared at me, but I didn't look away. After

a moment, his face paled, then flushed again, an angry mottled color.

"I am going to make you an offer," Tanek said. His voice was shaking now, but I was pretty sure it wasn't because he was scared. He might've been a coward, but at the moment, he was an angry coward.

"Why would you want to make a deal with me?" I asked even though I already knew the answer. Things were under his control right now, with just a few people knowing what had happened. He knew I had money, and probably suspected that I had connections. He didn't want to risk me using either of them to expose the truth.

"I am sure you do not want to put the princess through the humiliation of a trial."

I scowled and tasted fresh blood.

"Here is my deal. If you confess everything, I will convince the police to drop the charges. You will be deported and never allowed in Saja again."

"I think I'll take my chances in court," I said dryly. There was no way the king and queen would force Nami to go through with testifying.

"Is that so?" Tanek scowled. "If that is your decision, I will make sure that Namisa must testify, confess every little detail of what you did to her."

"You wouldn't." I took a step forward.

"I would," he said. "And I will ensure that the lawyer asks the most awful questions. How she felt with you inside her. If you made her climax while you raped her."

I felt the blood draining from my face. He would do it. He would force Nami to lie under oath, and not just lie but be humiliated as she did it. Even though I knew she would be doing it to save Halea, I knew how she would hate herself for doing what she felt like would be a betrayal.

"And the best part," he continued. "Is that, with such a small judicial system, and the king and queen having to oversee everything..."

Fuck. I hadn't realized that Nami's parents would have to be a part of it, much less in charge of it.

"It would be at least a year before you would have a court date." Tanek's eyes gleamed. "And you would be here the whole time. Wondering what I am doing to the princess in your absence..."

Damn him! My hands curled into fists.

I hated the idea of confessing to something I didn't do, especially something as hideous as rape. I hated that anyone would think I could hurt Nami that way, and I had a bad feeling Tanek would use it as another bit of blackmail, but it was much better than the alternative.

If I confessed, I'd be sent to the airport and then home to the US. I'd hire the best attorney possible and come back to Saja to fight the charges and save

Nami and her sister. While I didn't want to leave Nami with Tanek for another minute, it would still be less time than if I refused to confess and she was with Tanek until the trial. I shook my head. Even then, here'd be no guarantee I'd be free then either. In fact, if Nami lied – and with Halea at the mercy of Tanek, I had no doubt she would – I was almost certainly going to be found guilty. And most likely killed.

I just had to steel myself to do the lesser of two evils.

Chapter 10

Nami

I didn't want to take a shower and lose the lingering scent of Reed on my skin, but as soon as Claudel closed the door behind me, I headed straight for our bathroom. Tanek had said he would call a doctor to examine Halea and me. I didn't think he was lying about that. I wasn't sure how far he would go with these accusations against Reed, but I knew he'd want as much 'proof' as possible to hold over my head, and Reed's. The most obvious evidence would be Reed's DNA on and in me.

I scrubbed myself thoroughly, cleaning every inch until I was certain nothing of Reed lingered. As I stepped out of the shower, I wiped the fog off the mirror and forced myself to look. I needed to make sure there wasn't anything else on my body that could incriminate Reed. On the side of my neck was a small bruise, edged by what I knew were teeth marks. Heat flooded my body as I remembered the feel of him biting me. It wasn't too deep though and I doubted it would be enough for any sort of proof.

I touched it lightly and closed my eyes, letting myself remember Reed's touch, the feel of him on me, inside me. I knew Tanek would be back soon. Taunting Reed would keep him occupied for a bit, but I knew it was me he truly wanted to make pay. I had absolutely no delusions about what would happen when he got back.

The memory of Reed and what we'd shared last night would keep me strong, keep me sane. I opened my eyes. I just couldn't afford to spend too much time in my head. I needed to dress and then try to figure out what I would do next.

I couldn't just be passive about this anymore. I had to do something to save not only Halea, but myself. It wouldn't be tonight. I knew that. I'd resigned myself to what was going to happen to me, but I refused to think about it. Instead, I was going to start being proactive.

I dressed simply, knowing no matter what I wore, Tanek would be pissed. At least if he drew blood, it wouldn't ruin something good. I sat in a corner chair so I could see the door, not because I thought I'd be able to escape when it opened, but because I didn't want to be caught off guard. Now, it was time to plan.

By the time the door slammed open, a couple hours had passed and I wasn't any closer to figuring out what to do. I'd gone through all of the protocols I knew, all of the passages in and out of the house. Every person who might help me. Every time though, I couldn't figure out a way to make sure Halea was safe while I came up with the evidence to show my parents.

When I saw Tanek's face, however, an idea popped into my head. It was a bad one. Possibly the worst one I'd ever had. But it was all I had.

"Come here, you little bitch." Tanek was already moving towards me even as he spoke. He didn't want to give me a chance to obey.

I climbed off of the bed and, as he reached for me, I saw his knuckles were already bloody and bruised. "What did you do?"

He grabbed my hair, yanking my neck back far enough to make it hurt. "I did to him what I am going to do to you." He added, "Except fucking. I am not a pervert."

I didn't even bother to argue with the hypocrisy of a sadistic rapist referring to homosexuality as perverted.

He let go of my hair and I could see on his face that he was daring me to run, to try to get away. He wanted an excuse to hurt me more. I refused to give it to him.

He grabbed the collar of my shirt and tore it straight down the center. I was definitely glad I hadn't put Reed's t-shirt back on. I'd hidden it so it would be safe from Tanek's rage.

"Not even wearing a bra." Tanek grabbed my breasts, squeezing hard enough to make me gasp. "How long did it take before you spread your legs for him?"

One hand moved up to my throat, not squeezing tight enough to leave marks, but enough to keep me in place as he shoved his other hand down the front of my pants. His fingers were rough as they probed between my legs.

"Was he the one who took your virginity?" His fingers found my clit and pinched. "Was he?" he shouted.

I shook my head.

"Did you offer him your cunt in exchange for him taking you and your sister?"

I shook my head, tears coming to my eyes as he twisted the delicate bundle of nerves.

The hand in my pants came out and made a fist before I could think. He drove it into my stomach, but I couldn't bend over, held in place by the hand around my throat. His fingers tightened.

"Careful," I gasped when I finally had some breath. "Don't want to leave marks where my parents can see them."

He grinned at me. "That is the beauty of this punishment." His hand tightened again and I began to choke. "I can and will mark you wherever I please. I do not need to be careful. The doctor coming tomorrow will want to see all of them. After all, we must have a clear record of the injuries you sustained when you were assaulted by that horrible American."

He released my throat a moment before I passed out and I fell forward, gasping and coughing. I'd thought if I could get him to beat me, I could show my parents the marks as proof and have Tanek arrested before he could get to Halea. Now, I saw he'd already thwarted my plan, even without knowing it.

I barely realized Tanek was pulling off the rest of my clothes until he was pulling me up again and throwing me against the dresser. I collided with the side of it, the corner driving into my ribs. I felt blood running down my side, but didn't look down to confirm that the skin had broken.

"The police, the guards, Halea, they all know I was unmarked." I knew it was a stupid thing to say, but I had to try. I wasn't trying to avoid the beating, but reminding him that people knew the truth. I couldn't tell the doctor Reed had hurt me if there were those who could dispute it.

Tanek undressed as he stared at me, dropping

his clothes to the floor. His belt, however, he kept in his hand. "Police officers and security guards can have tricky memories if enough incentive is given."

My insides were trembling at the sight of that belt, but I didn't let him see it.

"As for your sister." He cracked the belt. "If she knows what is good for her, she will keep her mouth shut."

My eyes narrowed.

"And you will tell her that tomorrow when you see the doctor. You will convince her that she is to confirm everything you say."

I didn't say a word or make a sound as he brought the strap down on my side.

"You should also know that, should you ever attempt to run again, you should remember that I employ a great number of people who are my eyes and ears."

I turned as he brought the belt down two more times in quick succession, pain bursting across my back and ass.

Suddenly, he was there, pushing me against the dresser, his cock hard on my ass. He kicked my ankles apart as he grabbed my hair again, twisting my head so he could speak directly in my ear.

"And some of those employees are very well trained in finding missing people. Trust me, they would search to the end of the world in exchange for a piece of your sister's virgin pussy."

I froze, then dropped my head. It was over then. Even if I managed to get Halea away, we would never be safe. I barely flinched when Tanek thrust into my ass even though the pain tore through me. He was right. He could use me however he wanted without regard for how it looked tomorrow. In fact, the worse, the better.

He didn't last too long, but I knew that didn't matter. If he couldn't manage to go again, he'd use something else. He was far from done with me.

The belt came again, hard enough to leave welts. Once, he hit my cheek and I cried out. That's when I heard the door open.

"Princess..."

I barely had enough presence of mind to try to cover myself as Kai and Tomas stepped into the room. I watched their eyes go from me to Tanek and back again. The expressions on their faces, more than how I felt, told me how bad I looked.

"Leave," Tanek hissed. "Return to your duties with Princess Halea, or I swear I will kill Namisa and claim I saw you two do it."

They looked at me and I knew they would do whatever I said.

It wasn't even a question.

I needed my sister safe.

"Go to Halea," I said. My voice was hoarse.

"Keep her safe."

They left, but not before I saw the anger in their eyes.

The interruption seemed to have taken the majority of Tanek's anger and he tossed the belt away. "Slut."

I heard more than felt him spit on me, and then the door was closing and I was alone.

I wanted a shower, but I didn't want to move. I never wanted to move again. For the first time in my life, I actually considered how much easier it would be to just kill myself. I could almost feel it, a razor across my wrists, up my forearms. Blood pouring down my arms, releasing me, freeing me.

But then I remembered what Tanek had said he would do if I wasn't there. If I died, he would take my sister.

A felt a new kind of cold spread through me, something I hadn't felt before. This wasn't like ice. This was steel, hard and unbendable. The kind of cold I would need if I was going to protect Halea. The kind of cold I would need to kill Tanek.

Not in self-defense, not in a heat of the moment kind of thing. I was talking something calculated. Planned. First degree, cold-blooded murder. The kind of thing that could get me executed if I managed it. But it would mean Halea would be safe and I would be free.

My entire body pulsed with pain, but I pushed myself up, first onto my hands and knees. I stood, first leaning on the wall for support, and then managing it on my own two feet. First, a shower, and then, I would start figuring out the best way to kill my husband.

Chapter 11

Reed

I would've written my bogus confession right away if the cops had brought me a pen and paper. As it was, I didn't get either until mid-day on Sunday. I was pretty sure Tanek had told them to make me wait until then, wanting me to have to spend at least one night in jail. If I hadn't been so worried about Nami, I actually wouldn't have cared. The bed wasn't the most comfortable thing I'd ever slept on, but it wasn't too bad. I was alone in my cell, probably because Tanek didn't want me talking to anyone about what had happened, and I was unselfconscious enough that I didn't care about taking a piss out in the open.

But here I was, and that meant I spent Sunday writing out the most miserable piece of filth I'd ever seen. I tried being vague, simply writing that I'd met the princess in Paris, come to Saja and when I found her married, I'd kidnapped her. Halea had walked in so I'd taken her too. We'd gone to a hotel and I'd forced Nami to have sex with me.

I was sick to my stomach when I handed the paper to the officer, and then even more so when he gave it back.

"Prince Tanek was very clear. You must provide a detailed motive as well as be specific as to what you did to the princess." The cop looked almost as ill as I felt and I would've felt sorry for him if he hadn't been following the orders of a complete ass. At least it seemed like he thought he was doing the right thing.

I went back to the bed and sat down again. This time, I elaborated as to why I'd come to Saja, using at least some form of the truth in that regard. I said I'd fallen for the princess and wanted to court her. Then the lies started again. I said that when I found out she was married, I tried to make a pass at her and she rebuffed me. I was angry and decided that I would have her no matter what. I took her and Halea when the latter interrupted us.

I had to stop when I reached the part where I was supposed to elaborate on what I'd done to Nami. The moment I thought of putting pen to paper and coming up with lies as to how I'd violated her, my stomach heaved. I tossed the papers aside and barely made it to the toilet in time for my breakfast to come up.

I sat there for a few minutes, eyes closed, waiting to see if I was going to throw up again. I didn't want to do this, but I knew I had to. If I didn't do it exactly how Tanek wanted, he'd find some way to motivate me, and I didn't even want to think about what that would be. Plus, I knew the longer I was in jail, the more time he had to hurt Nami.

I stood, flushed the toilet then went to the sink and rinsed my mouth out. I splashed water on my face and looked in the mirror. One whole side of my face was swollen and bruised from where Tanek had hit me. It wasn't bad enough that I couldn't see clearly, but it wasn't comfortable either.

"Pull yourself together," I told my reflection. "You know what he's doing to Nami, and the only way you can help her is if you lie. Stop being such a pussy."

With that pep talk, I went back to the task at hand. As I began, I remembered how Nami had related Tanek's assaults to me, and I used what she'd said. When she and Halea were safe, I'd make sure this confession was brought out and the truth told about who had really done these things. Nami might not have filed a complaint against Tanek, but her experiences would be written down.

I finished and handed the confession over to the officer. He skimmed it and I watched the disgust and anger grow on his face. I wanted to tell him that it hadn't been me, that I'd never do anything like that to any woman, much less Nami, but I kept my mouth shut. My reputation wasn't important right now. Once the princesses were away from Tanek, I would consider everything else.

Finally, he nodded. "This will do. A car will be here in the morning to take you to the airport."

Tomorrow. One more day and I'd be out of here and on my way to figuring out how to save Nami.

I went back to the bed and stretched out. I knew I wouldn't sleep well tonight either. My brain was already buzzing with a thousand different plans, each more unlikely than the next. At least I had the rest of the day with uninterrupted silence to think.

When the cell door opened the next morning, I'd managed only a couple hours of sleep, none of it restful, and I wasn't any closer to figuring out what to do than I had been when I'd first started.

"Time to leave."

One of the cops who'd arrested me came into the cell, the expression on his face telling me that he fully believed the charges. He looked like he wanted nothing more than to finish what Tanek had started, but I wasn't about to give him an excuse to hit me. I stood and put my hands in front of me, making sure he could see that I wasn't going to try anything.

He grabbed my arm and yanked me towards the

door. I wanted to pull back, but I refrained. Just a little bit longer and I'd be free. A black town car was sitting in front of the station and the cop gave me a shove towards it.

"I pray you come back to Saja," he said. "It will give me great pleasure to make you suffer."

I was off to a great start, winning the hearts of Nami's people. I only hoped that when all was said and done, people like this police officer would understand why I'd done what I did.

I climbed into the back seat of the car, realizing for the first time how completely grimy I was. I was still wearing only the boxers they'd let me put on before leaving the hotel and I hadn't showered. I assumed this had been another way of Tanek trying to humiliate me. I grimaced at the smell. I couldn't get on a plane like this. If nothing else, I at least needed a shirt.

"Hey." I tapped on the black glass separating me from the driver. "I need to go to my hotel room and get my things."

No response.

"I at least need some clothes. They won't let me on a plane like this."

The window didn't come down, but I felt the car turn and slow.

Oh shit. A stab of panic went through me. I'd really thought that Tanek had meant to let me go.

Having me put on trial or killed while in police custody would've caused some serious international relations with America. My godfather was a retired Congressman who still had clout in Washington.

However, if I should happen to be found dead in a seedy part of the city – even in a place like Saja, there had to be some unsavory parts, right? – the victim of a robbery, it would be sad, but officials could say that they were doing everything in their power to bring the killers to justice. Even better, if they made it look like I'd been involved in something illegal – gambling, prostitution, drugs – they could almost guarantee that the US would stay out of it.

I heard both the front doors open and my heart began to pound. This was definitely not good. One person, I might be able to fight off, but not two, not on as little sleep as I'd had. Still, I tensed as the back door opened. I wouldn't give up without at least trying.

A familiar face looked in at me though it took me a moment to place it since the expression was actually friendly.

"Out."

I climbed out of the car, wondering why Kai and, I saw as I straightened, Tomas, had been chosen to escort me to the airport. Kai shut the door behind me and tossed me a shirt. My shirt, I saw with some surprise.

"Tanek has all of the family's cars under surveillance," Tomas said.

I pulled on my shirt. I would've felt better with pants too, but at least this was something.

"We know you are innocent of what Tanek says."

I stared at Kai. "What?"

"We have been assigned to Princess Halea, and she told us the truth of what happened," Tomas said. "The night the princesses returned, we went to see Princess Namisa, to ask her what she wished us to do in regards to Princess Halea's claims."

Kai's face tightened as he continued from where Tomas left off. "Tanek was beating Princess Nami."

My hands curled into fists.

"We wanted to stop him," Tomas said. "But he said he would kill the princess and frame us for the murder."

"Still, we would have tried," Kai insisted. "But Princess Nami told us to go to her sister."

I didn't doubt that. Even if she was being attacked, Nami's thoughts would've been to keep Halea safe.

"We spoke with the police," Tomas said. "And they told us you had written a confession. This was Tanek's doing?"

I nodded. "He said if I didn't, he'd make sure Nami had to testify to all sorts of horrible lies in front of her parents, and that I'd be waiting for a trial for a year, knowing that he was hurting her the whole time."

Tomas and Kai exchanged a look. It was Tomas who spoke, "Will you answer us honestly?"

I probably should have asked what the question was first, but I nodded instead. I was starting to suspect that Kai and Tomas wanted to protect Nami as much as I did.

"We know that you slept with Princess Nami in Paris and in Venice," Kai said.

"I did," I admitted, hoping this wasn't the part where they decided to kill me to avenge her honor. I didn't think so, but I could've been wrong.

"But then you came here for her," Tomas said.

"I did."

"Why?" Kai asked.

"Why?" I echoed.

"Why did you come here?" Tomas asked. "Paris and even Venice made sense, but lust does not inspire a man to come halfway around the world for a woman. Nor to risk what you have risked for her."

"I love her," I said. "I came here because I love her and I want to marry her."

"You have already put your freedom in jeopardy because of her," Tomas continued. "And now you have a free pass to go home. If you would like, we will drive you to the airport, as per our instructions."

"And if I don't like?" I asked.

"Then we would ask for your help," Kai said.

"Help with what?" I needed to hear the answer from them.

Tomas answered, "Help getting Princess Nami out of the country and away from Tanek."

Relief flooded through me. I wouldn't to have to do this alone. First, they had to know all of it. "We need to take Princess Halea too. That's how Tanek has been keeping Nami quiet. He's threatened to do to Halea what he's been doing to Nami." The words almost choked me.

The fury on the guards' faces made me take a step back.

"Tomas will take the car to the airport as planned," Kai said. "And then drive it back to the palace." He looked at me. "He will then meet us at my apartment where we will be planning." He pointed towards an older car sitting at the other end of the alley. "That is my car."

Tomas walked to the back of the car and opened the trunk. Inside were my bags. He pulled them out and set them on the ground next to me. "You will need proper clothing for us to do this." He frowned at me. "And a shower."

I sighed. "Tell me about it." I picked up my bags. "All right, let's do this."

Chapter 12

Reed

We didn't have a lot of time to plan, I knew, because as soon as Tanek realized I wasn't on the plane, he would know that Tomas and Kai were helping me, and there wouldn't be any doubt as to what they were helping me do. The last thing we needed was for Tanek to either call the police or to add more security around the girls. I was pretty sure he wouldn't do the former, not now that I had Kai and Tomas helping me. He knew they'd seen what he'd done to Nami and since they'd been her long-term bodyguards, their word would carry a lot more weight with the king and queen than mine would. In fact, if the king and queen had been in Saja, I would've been tempted just to go to them, but they wouldn't be back until Wednesday and we couldn't wait that long.

While we waited for Tomas to join us at Kai's

apartment, I took a shower and changed into clean clothes. When I came out of the bathroom, Kai had food waiting. By the time Tomas arrived, I was feeling relatively alert, though I gratefully accepted one of the energy drinks that Kai handed out as we settled around his small kitchen table.

Tomas took a drink and then spoke, "Shortly after the wedding, Tanek removed Kai and me from Princess Nami's detail. He convinced the king and queen that it would be better if Kai and I moved to protect Princess Halea as she would be coming of age. We assumed Princess Nami asked to have us moved because..." He hesitated and then shrugged. "Because of you and everything that happened when we were in Paris and Venice."

"Oh." I grimaced. "Sorry."

He shook his head. "We see now that it was not the princess. Tanek replaced half of the guards with his own men. I can see now that Tanek knew he would not be able to harm the princess while she was under our protection."

"You may have been able to arrange time alone with the princess," Kai said. "But we knew that was because she wished it. If she did not, we would have stopped you."

"And we would have stopped him," Tomas said.

"We'll stop him now," I said.

The men nodded.

"And you two being Halea's guards is going to work in our favor." A plan was slowly forming. "We need to get her away someplace safe before Nami will even consider leaving. If I have the two of you taking care of Halea, then I can just worry about Nami."

"It will not be enough to simply remove them from the palace," Tomas said.

"Yeah," I said dryly. "I figured that one out all on my own."

Tomas glanced at Kai and then looked at me. "One of the reasons we thought you would be able to help us is that you have resources that we do not."

Ah. Right. Money. A lightbulb went off. Not just money, but connections outside of Saja. I had the resources to get the princesses out of the country.

"I might need some help with connections, but I think I have an idea." I leaned back. "I know there's the one airport, but does it deal with private planes?"

They both nodded.

"Then here's what we're going to do," I said. "I'll pay for a private plane to be ready this evening. You find some excuse to get Halea out of the palace and get her to the airport. I'll follow with Nami. Once we're on the plane, you two can do whatever you can to make yourselves safe until we can get Tanek put away." I looked at Kai first and then at Tomas. "You know he's going to come after you."

"We know," Kai said.

"But we promised to protect the princess and we failed," Tomas said. "We will not fail this time."

I nodded. "Can you come up with something that won't make Tanek suspicious?"

"We will tell Halea that we're taking her someplace safe. She knows enough about what's going on to understand that the palace is not safe for her or her sister. We will have her tell the other guards that she wishes to go shopping for the king's birthday next week," Tomas said. "They will not wish to do that, so we will take her."

"That's good," I said. "What about Tanek? How do we make sure he doesn't interfere?"

"Most Monday evenings, Tanek spends the evening drinking the king's finest wine." Kai didn't even bother to try to disguise the contempt in his voice.

"Good," I said. "So we don't have to wait. While you two are getting Halea out of there, I'll go for Nami. I can get into her room."

Kai raised an eyebrow and my cheeks grew hot.

"She showed me that I can get in through the maid's quarters."

"I knew we should have locked those quarters up," Tomas said with a sigh. "But it does not matter. She is no longer in that room."

"What?"

"She and Tanek were moved to the bridal suite after the wedding." Tomas looked down, as if suddenly realizing that I might not want to hear that.

"Where's that?" I asked, my chest tightening. I didn't want to think about what had been happening in that room.

Kai stood and walked across the small apartment to a cluttered desk in the corner. He rummaged through some things and came up with a piece of paper and a pencil. He brought it back to the table and began to draw.

"A map will probably be easier than trying to give you directions," Kai said. A few minutes later, he slid the paper across the desk.

"Nice." I had to admit, I was impressed. This wasn't just some stick figure equivalent. Kai had added in enough detail that I felt confident I could get from the maid's quarters to Nami's new bedroom without much difficulty. Well, at least without getting lost. "Now, what about the guards?"

"Tanek has been keeping both princesses in their rooms, with guards posted at all times," Tomas said. He leaned over and pointed to the room Kai had marked. "The guards are usually stationed here. What they and Tanek do not know is that there is a side entrance that the servants use." He gave a hard smile. "Tanek does not care enough to pay attention to what the servants do, and the guards are new enough that they have not yet learned all of the palace." He traced a line around to where Kai had made an arrow. "This is where you will want to enter."

"Do I need a key?" I asked. "The last thing I need to happen is to get stuck outside her room because the door's locked."

Tomas reached into his pocket and pulled out a key. "This is the servants' key. It will open all of the side doors."

"All right," I said. I looked down at the map. I could have this memorized by this evening, no problem. There were two other things we needed to talk about though. "Is the service entrance still available for a way out?"

Tomas shook his head. "Once Tanek figured out that you used it to escape Friday night, he ordered double the guards and a sign in sheet to be used every time the gate is opened."

"Okay." I sighed and ran my hand through my hair. "So how do I get on and off the grounds without being seen?" That probably should have been my first question.

"They do not search my car," Tomas said. "I will drive us in and you will be in the trunk."

Oh, that sounded like fun.

"Instead of meeting at the airport, you will meet us in the garage," Tomas said. "You and Princess Nami can ride out in the trunk."

Both he and Kai looked mortified at the thought of putting me and Nami in the trunk. I wasn't sure if it was more the idea of the princess or the two of us being together that they thought was worse. It was a good idea though. More than that, it was the only idea we had.

"All right," I said. "I assume Nami can get us to the garage without any problem?"

Tomas nodded. "She knows more hidden doors and passageways than anyone."

That didn't surprise me.

"One more thing," I said. "I need to know how we're going to get rid of Tanek after the girls are safe."

"We will need evidence," Tomas said. "The king and queen will not merely accept the word of a foreigner, especially once Tanek presents them with the kidnapping and rape charges. The fact that you have the princesses again will support that."

"What about you two?"

"Tanek will claim that we are angry at being moved from Princess Namisa's detail," Kai said.

"So what we need is someone else who'll support what a horrible person Tanek is." Another idea popped into my head. "And I think I know exactly who we can call."

Forty minutes later, a familiar face showed up at Kai's door. She gave the bodyguards each a look and then turned her attention to me. We sat down and I quickly explained to her what I needed her to do.

"Let me see if I understand," she said once I'd finished. "You wish for me to approach the king and queen when they return to Saja and tell them what Tanek did to me?"

"Yes." I didn't see any point in trying to sugarcoat it.

"He will kill me and our daughter."

"No, he will not," Tomas said. "Kai and I will escort you to the king and queen personally and you will bring your daughter with you."

I reached over and put my hand on Ina's. "If you do this, we will make sure Tanek can't hurt anyone ever again." I paused, and then added, "And I will hire a lawyer to ensure that Tanek and his family pay child support for your daughter until she comes of age."

Ina's eyes narrowed. "Do you believe I can be bought?"

"No," I said calmly. "I think it would be a way of me showing my gratitude for your help and you getting what you deserve."

"And we will make sure Tanek gets what he deserves," Kai said.

114

We fell silent as we watched her think and consider her options. Then, finally, she nodded. "I will do this." There was a stubborn set to her jaw that told me she wouldn't go back on her decision. "And I will bring my...how do you say this in English?" She looked at Tomas and said something in their language.

"Insurance," he said.

"Insurance?" I asked.

Ina gave me a hard smile. "Yes, insurance. The papers that prove Tanek is my daughter's father."

For the first time since I'd been handcuffed, I felt true hope. This could work. This could really work. I had one more call to make. I just hoped that I truly did have at least two real friends left in Philadelphia.

Chapter 13

Reed

Ina gave Kai and Tomas her address and then headed home. They would, we decided, go from the airport to Ina's house. Tanek would never think to look for them there. By the time he figured out what was happening, it would be too late. The princesses and I would be safe in Philadelphia. Kai and Tomas would protect themselves and then they would protect her as they took her to the king and queen. She would tell them the truth about what had happened between her and Tanek, and then Kai and Tomas would share the rest. Once Tanek was arrested, Kai and Tomas would tell the king and queen where we were.

I just hoped they didn't get in trouble for not giving up that information right away. We didn't need the two of them in jail. Then again, I was sure that if it happened, Nami would be able to straighten things out once we got the Tanek situation taken care of. I had to force my thoughts away from what would happen after. I needed to think only about what would be coming one step after another. If I tried to push too far ahead, I'd lose focus and that could be bad.

The sun was starting for the horizon when I climbed into the trunk of Tomas's car. It was nicer than Kai's, so I was glad it was the one we were using. Kai's car would be left a few blocks from the airport so that he and Tomas could use it to get closer to Ina's house before walking the rest of the way. Tomas's car would remain at the palace while we took one of the town cars to the airport. As I curled up in the trunk and Tomas shut the lid, I did allow myself a moment to think about what it would be like to be tucked into a trunk around this size with Nami curled up next to me.

I felt us stop at the gates and thoughts of anything other than getting onto the grounds fled. I didn't realize I'd been holding my breath until I let it out as the car started to move again.

All right. I took another breath, slow and deep despite the musty smell all around me. The guys would pull into the employee garage which was around back and then they would head to Halea's room and I'd follow the directions I'd memorized. It was going to work, I told myself. It had to.

I blinked against the bright florescent lights as the trunk opened. Kai gave me a terse nod and then they were gone. I climbed out of the trunk and looked around. The garage was small and they'd parked near the main door so I didn't have to go far. When I opened the door, I found myself about half a dozen yards from the door I needed to get to. Fortunately, we'd timed things well enough that it was that perfect time between afternoon and evening, when everything was shadowed but the night lights hadn't yet come on. It was also the time when the day time staff were leaving and the night staff arriving. I'd thought this would mean double the number of people to avoid, but Kai and Tomas had told me that it was the opposite when the king and queen were gone. Things were more lax, and that would definitely be good for us.

I took advantage of that and managed to get to the door without being seen. Walking into the maid's quarters was starting to feel far too familiar, but I tried not to let it distract me. I went through the door using the key Tomas had given me. I managed to keep myself from looking at the bed when I passed it. I couldn't afford to be distracted by memories, either bad or good. I went through the door and down the hall, hating how slowly I had to move, staying close to the wall and checking constantly to make sure I was alone.

I didn't know how much time had passed by the time I saw the guards standing outside the doors I knew led to Nami's room. My heart was pounding so loudly that I knew the guards had to hear it and my shirt was sticking to my back, damp with sweat. I was so close.

I took a step forward, then froze as one of the guards started to turn towards me. Shit. I flattened myself against the wall as close as I could and prayed it would be enough. After several terrifying seconds, the guard turned again and I heard them talking. I heard Nami's name, but couldn't understand anything else. It didn't matter though. As long as they weren't talking about a plan to free the princesses, I didn't care. And considering they weren't getting on their radios and panicking, I felt pretty safe in assuming they didn't know I was there.

Once I was sure they weren't going to look at me, I went around the corner and down the short hallway to where the servant's door was tucked away. My hand was shaking as I took the key out of my pocket and I realized that I was scared. Not of being caught, not of being arrested again. No, I was terrified to see Nami again and have her think that I'd failed her. I couldn't bear to look her in the eyes and see that she was disappointed with me for not being able to save her before, knowing that every pain she'd endured since I'd been arrested was my fault.

I took a slow breath and my hand steadied. As I put the key in the lock, I heard a thud from inside. I frowned. Had Nami dropped something? It hadn't really sounded like that though. Not a sharp sound. More dull. Almost like...

My heart leaped into my throat and adrenaline dumped into my veins. Another thump, this one accompanied by a sound of pain.

Nami.

I didn't even think about the guards or my own safety. I shoved the door open and stepped inside.

Tanek held Nami against the wall, gripping her arm with one hand, fingers buried in her flesh. The other hand was in the air, ready to hit her again. She had a red handprint on her cheek, but I could see bruises from where I stood. She was covered with them. The thin nightgown she was wearing did nothing to cover them. Not the ones on her arms. Not the welts on her shoulders that I knew had come from a belt.

I was going to kill him.

Chapter 14

Nami

I'd thought I'd get a reprieve from Tanek tonight. With my parents gone, he could raid the best of my father's alcohol without the risk of being caught. He had done that, but had apparently decided that he preferred coming to me rather than passing out wherever he'd sat down to drink.

Evenings at the end of June were warm and I'd finally turned on the air conditioning just enough to take the edge off. I'd chosen a fairly thin cotton nightgown, believing that I would be alone. I hadn't looked in the mirror though. I'd made the mistake of doing that yesterday morning when I'd gotten out of the shower. The memory was enough to make me cringe and I'd never been so glad not to have inherited my mother's fairer skin.

Tanek had staggered into the room just a few minutes ago, his face flushed. I'd considered running since he didn't look sober enough to come after me, but I'd known that would end just as badly because the guards would catch me, even if Tanek couldn't. The thought had flickered through my mind then that this was the time to fight back. I wasn't sure if I could do it though, and I knew that if I was going to kill Tanek, I had to be sure. I couldn't go halfway or I'd be the one dead.

Despite him being drunk, Tanek was still taller than me and outweighed me by enough to make a difference. I couldn't do it now. It had to be planned, not impulsive, or it would never work.

"Surprised to see me?"

I didn't say anything. It didn't matter how I answered him, he'd take it as an insult or find some fault in it. Nothing I said would stop him if he wanted to hit me, and he always wanted to hit me. Sometimes, I was actually glad that he wasn't one of those men who acted sorry afterwards and apologized. If he continued to abuse me, I preferred he just be a bastard all the time.

"Who are you wearing that for?" Tanek sneered. He grabbed my arm and gave me a shake. "I know it can't be for Reed. He left this morning."

I pressed my lips together to keep from asking the question I knew he wanted me to ask.

He answered anyway, still too drunk to manage English, "I offered to let him go if he confessed.

124

Didn't even take him long to decide."

My stomach fell. I should've been happy, I knew. Reed was free. He was on his way back to America where he would be safe. I couldn't help but feel a pang of betrayal that he'd been so easily swayed.

He smiled. "I've got the written confession right here. Handwritten and the only copy, of course. We don't need anything out there for nosy reporters to see...unless I want them to." He patted the pocket of his pants. "Do you want me to read it to you?" He thought for a moment. "No, better that I act it out first so you can be surprised. I'll read it to you after so you can relive the whole thing."

I glared at him but didn't say a word as he spun me around, shoving me against the wall with a dull thud. The welts on my back throbbed painfully as I hit the wall, but I kept quiet. I couldn't, however, stop the small sound of pain when he slapped me, his fingers landing on a place that had been bruised by his belt the night before.

He raised his hand to hit me again and I clenched my teeth, determined that he wouldn't get another sound out of me. He didn't get the chance to bring his hand down as the servants' door at the back of the room suddenly swung open.

For one long second Reed stood in the doorway, fury burning on his face like nothing I'd ever seen before.

125

He hadn't left me. He'd come back. Again. After all I'd put him through, he'd still come for me. I could see the bruising on his face, the exhaustion in every limb.

The relief rushing through my body came with something else. Anger. No, nothing so tame as anger. This was rage. Not only for what Tanek had done to me, but for what he'd done to Halea, what he'd done to Reed.

I was so done with his shit.

Remembering something I'd learned years ago in a self-defense class I'd insisted on taking before going to college, I jabbed my free hand at Tanek's throat, keeping my fingers stiff as they came in contact. Even as I did it, I brought my knee up as well. I heard the seams of my nightgown tear, but I didn't care. Shocked by the sudden blow to the throat – and not helped by the alcohol he'd consumed – Tanek couldn't think fast enough to protect his crotch. I felt a vindictive stab of satisfaction as my knee made direct contact.

Tanek dropped, his hand unable to hold my arm as he fell to his knees. He curled up, hacking and gasping, unable to make any noise loud enough to let the guards outside know that it wasn't me who was in pain.

I didn't even spare him a look as I ran straight into Reed's arms. His mouth came down on mine more gently than I wanted and I pressed myself against him, not caring that the kiss hurt my bruised lips. I buried my hands in his hair, twisting my fingers until Reed made a noise in the back of his throat and his arms finally tightened around me the way I wanted. My injuries throbbed painfully, but they were nothing compared to the joy I felt at being where I belonged. Heat flooded me, pushing aside all of the pain until all I could feel was him.

I wanted to stay there in his arms, forget everything else, but I could hear Tanek wheezing on the floor and I knew we didn't have time. I broke the kiss, allowing myself a moment to close my eyes, to feel safe for the first time since I'd fallen asleep in his arms. Then I stepped back.

"Oh, baby." Reed's voice was soft.

I looked up into those dark eyes and my heart did a little skipping beat at the emotion I saw there. Anger. Desire. Compassion. He brushed his fingers down the side of my face, light enough that it didn't hurt.

"I could say the same." I placed a gentle hand on his injured cheek. "But I'm okay."

He raised an eyebrow as he reached up and took my hand. "This is far from okay."

"You're here," I said.

"I am." He glanced at Tanek. "And that fucking bastard will never touch you again."

"Halea..." My heart constricted.

"Safe," he said. He lowered his voice so that Tanek couldn't hear him. "Kai and Tomas are getting her."

I breathed a sigh of relief.

"This has to be your choice, Nami." He squeezed my hand. "I want you to come with me. You and Halea. Come to the States, where I can protect you."

"Go...back?" I don't know why that came as a surprise. It made sense. Quite a bit, actually. Reed had connections that could keep us safe until we figured out what to do. Then I realized he was still waiting for an answer. "Yes. Of course, yes."

He smiled. "Let's go."

"*Bitch.*" Tanek's voice was little more than a croak.

I stopped mid-step. Reed gave me a concerned look. "I can't leave in this." I gestured as I pulled my hand away from his. "Will you get me something to wear?"

As he moved to do as I asked, I walked back over to where Tanek was laying. He was trying to get back up, his mouth working as he was trying to get sounds out. I knew the chances of him calling the guards was about fifty-fifty at the moment. He wanted to hurt me, beat me, maybe to death. And he didn't want anyone to know that a woman had put him down. But, I knew if he thought Reed and I were going to get away, he'd risk it, probably lie to the guards and tell them that Reed had done it.

I wasn't going to risk it.

I looked down at Tanek as he started to push himself up against the wall. All of the rage I'd pushed down, the humiliation, the pain, I let it come up. My hand curled into a fist. I was done. Done being beaten.

"Fuck you!" I put all of my weight behind the swing. Pain flared up my knuckles and my arm, jarring and bright, but it was worth it to see Tanek's head spin around, hear his strangled cry.

His eyes were dazed as he looked up at me, but he couldn't keep himself upright. As he slumped down on the floor, I drew back my foot and kicked him in the stomach, ignoring the sharp pain in my toes. He retched and I pulled back again.

"Nami." Reed grabbed my arm and I looked up at him. His eyes were hard. "You shouldn't do that without shoes." He held up a pair of slip-on tennis shoes. "You could hurt yourself."

I pulled on the shoes and then reached for the dress he'd pulled from my closet. I didn't look down at Tanek who was still coughing and whimpering. I pulled the nightgown over my head, stiffening as I heard Reed swear under his breath, but I didn't look at him either. I pulled the sundress over my head, thankful that Reed had picked something that wasn't

129

too rough against my bruises.

"I'm going to kill him." Reed's eyes were as dark as I'd ever seen them. Pitch black and full of something I'd never seen before. Hate. Not just anger, but pure hate.

"No." I grabbed Reed's arm. "We're not going to kill him." I didn't mention the fact that I'd been thinking of doing just that. Now that Reed was here, I didn't need to do that. Besides...I looked down at Tanek. "Death's too good for him."

I let go of Reed's arm and kicked Tanek again, this time without hurting my toes. He retched again, this time vomiting up whatever he'd been drinking. I made a face but reached down anyway and grabbed him by the hair.

"I will make sure you spend every moment of the rest of your life regretting you ever thought you were good enough to marry me." I hesitated for only a moment before I slammed his head against the floor. His eyes rolled up, body going limp. I dug into his pants and pulled out the envelope before I straightened and turned towards Reed. "Let's go."

Reed's eyes were wide as he stared at me. I waited for him to say something, anything, but he didn't. Instead, I watched two different emotions play across his face. Shock at what I'd done. And admiration. He held out his hand.

"We need to get to the garage. The one where

your family's cars are."

I nodded. We'd lost time that I was sure we needed. Tanek's guards wouldn't worry if they didn't hear anything or if Tanek didn't come out soon, but when he did wake up, we'd want to be as far away as possible.

We went back out the servants' door, but instead of going back towards the main hallway, I led Reed the other way. It looked like a dead end, but I knew it wasn't. Most of the big rooms had servants' entrances, which were common knowledge. The new guards Tanek had hired didn't know yet, but other members of the security team did. No one but family knew where we were going. And Tanek wasn't family enough for this.

Saja was a peaceful country, but when my great-great-great-grandfather had built the new palace, World War II had been enough of a reality for him to worry about his family. He'd had hidden passages built throughout the house. Even generations later, we'd kept the secret, and now I was glad we had.

I found the panel easily and pressed my fingers into the release. I heard a small sound of surprise but didn't look back. I felt along the wall and found the flashlight we kept inside. The beam was fairly weak, but it was enough. I listened hard as we walked, waiting for any sound that would indicate Tanek had woken up.

I slowed as we passed another panel that should lead to the hallway just outside the kitchen, which meant that the next one would be the garage. I had an idea of what the plan was. If Kai and Tomas were getting Halea, that meant they were probably planning to take us all out in one of my family's cars. How we were going to manage that without being seen by the outside guards, I didn't know, but I trusted Reed and the guys. They would get us out of here.

I pushed the release and the panel slid aside. Reed stepped in front of me before I could walk out, bending his arm so that he pulled me close to his back, shielding me with his body. A surge of love went through me, so strong that it brought tears to my eyes. Tanek had used and abused my body for his own pleasure, and even though the last time had cost him his freedom, Reed continued to put himself between me and any threat.

"Nami!"

Reed let go of my hand and moved out of the way so that Halea could run into my arms. I clutched her tightly, looking over her head at Reed. "Thank you." I wanted to keep looking at him, but there were two others I needed to thank as well. I slid my eyes over to Kai and Tomas and repeated the same words to them. They nodded.

"What did he do to you?" Halea's words were

muffled and I reluctantly released her. Her eyes were wide and concerned, though I could see the anger underneath it.

"Don't worry about it." I started to tuck her hair behind her ear but stopped when she scowled at me. Shit. She was angry at me.

"Why didn't you tell me it was this bad," she demanded. "Nami..." Her bottom lip trembled and tears welled up in her eyes. "Why didn't you..." Her voice trailed off and I watched things click. "Me. You stayed because of me." She looked at the guys and then back at me. "That's why I had to go with you last time. Not because you were just afraid he was violent in general. Tanek threatened me, didn't he?"

"Nami." Reed's voice was soft. "You may have knocked the bastard out, but we still need to go."

"You did what?" Halea was startled into English.

I lifted my chin. "I gave him back a little of what he gave me."

"Good," Halea said. The anger in her voice surprised me.

"Princesses," Tomas spoke, an urgent tone in his voice. "We need to go."

"Right." I turned towards my former bodyguards. "How are we doing this?"

Tomas opened the trunk to one of the town cars. "I am sorry."

If I hadn't seen the look of chagrin on Tomas's

face, I wouldn't have believed it.

"We told the other guards we are taking Halea shopping for your father's birthday," Kai said.

"Which means she can sit in the car," I realized. "But I can't." I looked at Reed. "And neither can you."

He shrugged, his expression blank but his eyes dancing. "It'll be a snug fit, but I think we can manage."

I was surprised at the sudden flare of arousal that went through me. Even with all that had happened, the thought of being crammed into a tight space with Reed...I wanted him. It may have been crazy, but I couldn't help it.

My throat tightened when I saw the same desire shining in Reed's eyes.

"It'll make more sense if I get in first."

I wasn't sure if anyone else noticed the rough edge to Reed's voice, but my body certainly recognized it. I watched as Reed climbed into the trunk and then climbed in after him. As Tomas closed the lid, I settled back against him.

"Is it okay if I put my arms around you?" Despite the desire I could feel radiating off him, Reed sounded almost hesitant.

"Please." I leaned my head back so that it was resting on his shoulder. I sighed as his arms went around my waist.

Neither of us spoke again until we knew we'd passed through the front gate and were on our way to the airport. When Reed did break the silence, what he said wasn't what I'd expected.

"What's in the envelope?"

I'd completely forgotten about the envelope until now, and was almost surprised that I still had it. "Oh, that." I couldn't turn to look at him, but I held it over my shoulder so he could take it. "It's your...confession." I put as much derision into the word as I could."

"Really?"

"That piece of shit got this from the police so he could show it to me. It is the only copy."

Reed chuckled, surprising me again. He kissed the top of my head. "You are the most amazing woman, Namisa Carrmoni." His arms tightened briefly around me. "I love you."

Four words didn't seem adequate to express everything I was feeling, but they were all I had at the moment. "I love you too."

Chapter 15

Reed

I grimaced as my vertebrate made loud popping sounds. I stretched my arms above my head and twisted my waist. Being crammed into a trunk two times in a short period of time wasn't exactly friendly on the spine or muscles, no matter how pleasant the companionship had been the second time.

I glanced at Nami and then looked away. I was already half-hard from being pressed tight against her. Continuing to look at her was either going to give me an uncomfortable erection for the plane ride or piss me off. The bruises I'd first seen on her when I'd walked into her room had been bad enough, but then she'd taken off the dress and I'd wanted to beat Tanek to death. There wasn't an inch on her that didn't have a new or at least fading bruise. The only thing that had kept the bastard alive was that Nami had stopped me. I promised myself that I would do whatever it took to make sure Tanek spent the rest of his life as another inmate's bitch.

"Mr. Stirling?"

I turned as the pilot approached. He wasn't anyone I knew, but I'd chartered private jets through this particular international company before and I knew them to be professional and, more importantly, discreet. Right now, the most important thing was to keep as many details as possible quiet for as long as we could.

"My name is Antonio Russo." He flashed impossibly white teeth when he smiled. "I will be flying your party to a private airstrip just outside of Padua. Another plane will be waiting to complete your trip to the United States."

I shook his hand. "Thank you. Are we ready to go?"

"Yes, Sir." Antonio nodded. "Whenever you are."

"We'll board in a minute," I said. "I just need to have a few words with the gentlemen who won't be coming with us."

The pilot nodded again and then picked up the luggage Kai had pulled from the backseat. I gave the bodyguard a surprised look. I hadn't even thought about my things. I was glad he had though. It was one less thing I had to bother with.

"Princess Namisa," Tomas spoke, his voice

surprisingly emotional. "Before you leave, we must beg your forgiveness."

Nami's eyes widened in surprise, but she didn't say anything.

"Kai and I had been charged with keeping you safe for years and we have failed in our duty."

"No." She shook her head. "The blame for this lies on no one but Tanek Nekane. You protected my sister. You made sure that she was not harmed by my husband. There is nothing to forgive."

Kai opened his mouth as if he'd protest, but a sharp look from Nami stopped him.

"Now we have to finish what we have started," she said. She looked over at me. "I am assuming that running to Philadelphia is not the end of the plan."

"It's not," I said. "I'll give you the details on the plane, but the short version is that Kai and Tomas are staying here to implement the last part of the plan to get Tanek arrested." I glanced at the plane. "We need to go."

"Reed is correct," Tomas said. He gave a bow to Nami and then to Halea before turning to me and holding out a hand. "Thank you."

"Thank you," I repeated. "And you two be careful."

"We will." Kai shook my hand as well. "Take care of our princesses."

"I will," I promised.

The pair got back into the town car and drove off to wherever they intended to hide it. After that, they'd go to Kai's car and head for Ina's apartment. Then it became a waiting game for them until the king and queen returned. For the princesses and myself, our time of waiting was beginning right now.

I held out a hand to Nami and she took it, then put her other arm around Halea. Together, we headed for the plane.

I hadn't bothered to ask for their nicest one since availability was more important, so it was more compact than some of the others I'd used before to entertain business associates, but it was still better than a commercial flight, even in first class. I'd been thinking of needing privacy because of who Halea and Nami were, but after seeing the marks on Nami's body, I was doubly glad I'd gone with private flights. The last thing she needed was people staring at her injuries.

Halea settled in one of the seats and, after a quick look at me, Nami went to sit beside her. I was a bit disappointed that she wasn't sitting with me, but I could see why she needed to be near her sister. I headed up to the cockpit to let the captain know we were ready to go and then went to the bar to find out what sort of drinks they had to offer.

By the time we touched down in Italy, both princesses seemed to be calmer and I'd finally started to relax as well. That, I assumed, had just as much to do with the couple of now-empty bottles of liquor I'd consumed. It wasn't enough for me to be drunk or even tipsy, but they'd definitely taken the edge off. I wouldn't be completely tension-free until we were home, but Italy was definitely safer than Saja. Kai and Tomas had assured me that, while relations with Italy were good, Tanek would still have to go through a process to try to get Nami and Halea back from there. It'd be even harder once we were in the States, and that would be if he could find us at all. Considering I trusted the only two people who knew we were coming, I doubted Tanek would be able to figure out where we were before the king and queen arrived back in Saja.

The plane in Italy was a little bigger than the first and included a long seat that Halea immediately claimed. As soon as we were airborne and allowed to unbuckle, Halea stretched out, falling asleep in seconds. I found a blanket and covered her with it, tucking it in so it wouldn't fall off. She looked even younger and more innocent, and I felt a surge of anger that Tanek could even consider hurting her.

"He's never going to touch you," I promised quietly. I knew she couldn't hear me, but that didn't matter. Even if the king and queen refused to lock up Tanek, I would do whatever it took to protect Halea and Nami.

"Reed." Nami slipped her hand into mine.

I turned around and looked down at her. I used my free hand to tuck an unruly curl behind her ear. "I don't care what it takes. I will make you safe again."

She raised herself on her toes and pressed her lips against mine. It was a fairly quick, chaste kiss, but I saw the bright flare of arousal in her eyes.

"You will do anything to make me feel safe?"

That wasn't exactly how I'd worded it, but it was close enough. "Yes."

One side of her mouth quirked up in a partial smile. "Good. Come with me."

I was confused, but let her pull me after her. As soon as I realized where she was going, I knew what she wanted. At least, I thought I did, even though I had to be wrong. What I was thinking was crazy.

"Do you know when I feel the most safe?" she asked as she opened the door to the bathroom. She backed inside and pulled me towards her. "When you are inside me."

Fuck.

"I don't know, Nami," I protested weakly.

She reached around me and closed the door, locking it. This bathroom was slightly larger than the one on a commercial plane, but it was still a tight fit.

"Do you want me?" she asked, reaching up to trace my bottom lip with her finger.

142

Chapter 16

Nami

I wasn't sure when I managed to fall asleep, but with Reed's arms around me and my head on his shoulder, it didn't surprise me. With the exception of that one night in the hotel, I'd only been sleeping in fits and starts since I'd met Tanek. An hour here and there, waking suddenly with a pounding heart and the certainty that Tanek was there in the dark. In Reed's arms, with his scent around me, the memory of him throbbing between my legs, I was able to let myself go. Even in sleep, when the darkness tried to frighten me, I knew he was there and the thought was enough to keep the demons at bay.

"Nami." His voice was soft in my ear, but loud enough to pull me from sleep. "We're almost home."

For a moment, I felt panic and my eyes opened. Then I realized what he meant and the fear faded, though the adrenaline had made me suddenly and completely awake. Reed gave me a concerned look as I sat up.

I didn't give him a chance to ask if I was okay. I had a feeling I would be sick of that question very soon. "Did you sleep at all?" I asked him.

He nodded. "A bit, but I don't think I'll really relax until we're in a place I know no one can get to you." He reached out and put his hand on my cheek, his touch light enough that it didn't hurt.

"Where are we going?" I asked suddenly, realizing I didn't know any details.

"Philadelphia," he said. "I have some friends there I can trust."

"Friends, not family?" I put my hand on his arm.

"No," he said. "I can't try to work things out with them and worrying about you at the same time."

"I don't want you worry about me or Halea," I said.

He gave me the kind of smile that said I just didn't understand. "You're my world, Nami. How can I not worry about you?"

Before I could think of something to say, he was on his feet and heading for the cockpit.

"I like him." Halea sat down next to me. Her face was pale and she looked tired even though I knew she'd slept through most of the eight hour flight. She reached over and took my hand. "I know you think you have to protect me, but I am stronger than you think."

I smiled as I squeezed her hand. "It wasn't your strength I doubted. It was mine. I could bear what Tanek did to me, but I couldn't have handled anything happening to you."

Tears spilled over, running down Halea's cheeks and she buried her head against my chest, her arms wrapping around me so tightly that it hurt. I didn't ask her to stop, putting my own arms around her and kissing the top of her head. My own eyes burned with tears.

"It's all right now, little one," I murmured. "Shh. We're safe now."

By the time Reed came back to tell us that we'd be landing at a private airstrip just outside of Philadelphia in a few minutes, Halea and I had both regained our composure enough to excuse ourselves to freshen up. I returned to my seat just as the pilot announced that we needed to put on our seat belts. I sat next to Reed. Now that the immediate concerns were out of the way and we were now simply waiting to hear from Kai and Tomas about my parents, I found myself growing nervous. Not at what was going to happen with Tanek, but rather what would be waiting for us in Philadelphia.

"Your friends," I asked as the plane began to descend. "Are they picking us up at the airport?"

"They are." Reed reached over and laced his fingers between mine. A faint flush stained his cheeks. "Do you remember me telling you about Piper?"

It took me a moment, but then I placed the name. "The woman whose decision to go with another man sent you to Europe?"

The corner of Reed's mouth twitched and his ears began to turn red. "I wouldn't have put it exactly like that, but yes. She and her boyfriend are picking us up. They moved in together earlier this summer, but she has an apartment in Fishtown that still has a lease on it. She hasn't been able to find someone to sublet it to, so we can stay there as long as we need to."

"That's very generous of her." I hoped I didn't sound suspicious, but I found it strange that a woman who'd rejected Reed would go to all this trouble to help him.

"Nami, there's nothing between Piper and me but friendship."

I looked up at Reed and found his expression serious. He raised our hands and kissed the back of mine.

"She's actually the one who told me that if I loved you, I needed to go after you and not let anyone stop me." He squeezed my hand. "What Piper and I had...it wasn't real. She and Julien are meant to be together." His eyes were warm as they met mine. "Just like we are."

Because of the six hour or so time difference, it was a little past one in the morning as we left the airplane and I shivered as a gust of wind whipped across the landing strip. Reed slid his arm around my waist and pulled me against him as we walked towards the couple who were waiting next to a normal-looking car. That was surprising. I'd assumed that Reed's friends had as much money as he did.

I looked at her first. She was about my age, maybe a year or two older. Bright red hair that she had pulled back in a ponytail. Dark green eyes and a light dusting of freckles across her fair skin. She was quite pretty, but the way she looked at the man standing next to her kept me from being jealous. She was clearly in love. He was tall with black hair and bright blue eyes, a handsome man, I thought, but not my type.

"Thank you guys so much for helping us," Reed said as we reached his friends. He put out his free hand and shook Julien's hand. Piper came forward to give him a half-hug, then gave me one as well, surprising me enough that I couldn't cover it.

She smiled. "Julien and I both know what it's like to have everything working against you." She reached behind her and he took her hand. "Any way we can help, we're more than happy to."

"Thank you," I said. All of the anxiety I'd had at meeting her melted away. She had one of the most sincere faces I'd ever seen. "I'm Nami and this is my sister Halea." I gestured towards Halea who gave Piper a shy smile. I purposefully left off our titles, though I supposed Reed had told his friends who we were. I didn't want them to think of us that way though.

"We brought the car rather than having someone drive us," Julien spoke up. "Figured it would be the best way to keep from drawing attention." He glanced at me and offered an additional explanation. "The apartment's not in a bad neighborhood or anything, but a town car would be noticed, even this early in the morning."

"Thank you," I said again.

He opened the back door and I climbed in while Halea walked around to the other side. Reed got in beside me as his friends put Reed's luggage in the trunk and then got into the front of the car.

As Julien began to drive, Piper half-turned in her seat so she could see us while she talked.

"You asked us to keep an ear out for any international news," she said to Reed. "There hasn't been anything yet." She looked at me, her expression open and compassionate. "I am so sorry for what happened to you."

I didn't know how much Reed had told her, but I knew at least some of the evidence was still clear on my skin. I nodded, swallowing hard. Reed put his arm around my shoulders. My stomach flipped and I closed my eyes for a moment, fighting a sudden wave of nausea. It was jet lag, I told myself. Jet lag and nerves. I'd been sick every day since Reed had been arrested.

"The place is mostly empty," Piper was saying. "We wanted to keep it furnished in case we had a renter who preferred it that way, but it's pretty plain. I went over right after we got off the phone and cleaned, then went shopping."

I opened my eyes and caught Halea looking at me, concerned. I managed a smile and turned my attention to the city I could see through the windshield. We didn't go downtown though, heading off to a neighborhood outside what I would have considered the city. Piper informed us that Fishtown was part of Philadelphia, but not the business or historical district. I was going to ask why they called it Fishtown when one of the streetlights illuminated the image of a fish on the side of one of the buildings. Not like a drawing or anything like that, but rather a metal cast. I couldn't see much detail as we passed, but it was enough to confirm it was a fish.

"Here we are," Julien said as he pulled up to the

curb.

We were on a cobblestone street off of the main one, parked in front of what I would have thought of as a row house rather than an apartment. It was a rustically beautiful red brick building. I was sure it would be even nicer looking in the daylight.

Piper went up the steps and unlocked the door while Julien grabbed Reed's bags. He kept his arm around me as we followed Piper and Halea followed us. We stepped into a living room just as Piper flicked a switch, lighting things up. It had been painted fairly recently, I saw. Not enough that we could smell it, but enough for it to be clear that she'd done some work on the place.

"It's lovely," I said.

"Thank you." Piper gave me a warm smile. "I brought over some clothes for you to wear if you needed them. They're upstairs in the main room. Linens are in the hall closet just outside the bathroom. The fridge is stocked with food and drinks."

"You didn't have to do all of that," Reed said.

"Yes, I did." Piper turned her smile on him, but it was clear it was only platonic. "You did so much for me, it was the least I could do."

"It's late," Julien spoke up. "We'll leave you to get settled. Give us a call if you need anything, no matter the time."

"Thank you." Reed put out his hand again and Julien shook it.

The three of us stood in silence for nearly a full minute after Piper and Julien left. The apartment was quiet and any sounds from outside were muffled. Reed released me to walk over to the door and turn the deadbolt. I had a feeling he wasn't doing it because he thought we needed protection from people in the neighborhood.

"Why don't you two head upstairs," he said. "I'll see what Piper has in the kitchen and whip us up something while you're showering. When you're done, I'll bring up some food and take a shower. There are two bedrooms. The bigger one's on the right. I'll be in the one on the left."

"No," Halea spoke up. "You and Nami will share the bigger room."

"Halea." I could feel the heat burning in my cheeks.

"I am not a child, Namisa." Halea's eyes narrowed and, for the first time, I saw myself in her face. "You two need to be together. End of discussion."

As she started up the stairs, Reed turned to me with a half-smile on his face. "That is definitely your sister."

I laughed softly. "Yes, she is." I held out my hand. "Shall we find something to eat before going upstairs to our room?" I liked the sound of that.

He took my hand and then sighed.

"What's wrong?" I asked.

"We finally get a room where we won't be interrupted and I'm too tired to do anything but sleep."

I laughed again and stepped into him, wrapping my arms around his waist. His automatically closed around me as well. I rested my cheek on his chest. "That's okay. We have plenty of time. And falling asleep in your arms sounds like the best thing in the world right now."

He kissed the top of my head. "Yes," he agreed. "It does."

Chapter 17

Reed

Waking up in that bed, with Nami in my arms, the bright sunlight streaming in between the curtains, the smell of whatever it was Halea was cooking wafting up the stairs, it was like something out of a dream.

Piper had left some of her clothes for the girls and I still had a clean outfit or two in my bags, but it was pretty clear that one of the first things we needed to do after breakfast that morning was go shopping.

I called a car and the three of us went into the city. There still hadn't been anything on the news about the girls being missing and I was beginning to suspect that there wouldn't be. Tanek still had until tomorrow evening before the king and queen knew something was wrong, I was willing to bet that he would do whatever it took to make sure they didn't find out. That probably meant he'd try to figure out where we'd gone and come after us. I just hoped that by the time he realized we'd left the country, Kai and Tomas would have gotten Ina to the king and queen.

I wasn't going to worry about that though. We were safe for now and it was Nami's first time in Philadelphia, and Halea's first time in the United States. I may have had issues with my family and some of the members of Philadelphia high society, but I did love my city and I intended to show it off. We went to Macy's first, so the girls could get clothes and so that I could see the expressions on their faces when they saw the gigantic pipe organ that covered the upper parts of the walls.

When we left a couple hours later, we had enough clothes to last all three of us several weeks. We took them back to the apartment and then went out to walk. The weather was absolutely gorgeous. A bit hot considering it was the end of June, but there was a nice breeze and I could tell that the freedom of being out and about without having to worry about bodyguards or anything like that made the air smell twice as sweet.

The three of us spent the rest of Tuesday and all of Wednesday in various parts of the city. We walked and ate and talked. Halea quickly became enough at ease with me that she didn't seem self-conscious anymore, and even tried teaching me some of their native language. Nami's face lost its look of pinched worry and she began to get her color back even as her bruises faded. She still looked a bit peaked in the mornings, but I wasn't worried. It would take awhile for her frayed nerves to mend. We didn't know how long our peaceful time together would last, but none of us talked about it. We wanted to enjoy what we had and not think about anything else. When things started to change, we'd deal with it, but for the moment, we were safe and happy.

Thursday morning, we were up early and in the kitchen discussing what we'd be doing after breakfast when someone knocked on the door. Immediately, the mood shifted. Julien and Piper both had keys, and although they might knock just to be polite, something in my gut said that it wasn't either of my friends.

"Stay here." I was technically talking to both of them, but I looked at Nami. Halea would follow her sister's lead, and I didn't want Nami doing something foolish.

Nami raised her eyebrow but didn't argue. I took that as agreement and went out as the person at the door knocked again.

I could've asked who it was, but it'd end up the same either way. If, by some strange fluke, it was Tanek, he wouldn't be getting into the house, no matter who was with him. American police wouldn't come in without a warrant or an invitation. And if

Tanek himself tried, I'd yell for Nami to call the police.

As soon as I opened the door, however, everything changed. It wasn't Tanek on the other side, or any of the bodyguards. It wasn't even the American police, called by Tanek, which was something I'd had in the back of my mind.

No, the two people standing on the doorstep were familiar-looking. And the last two people I would've expected to see standing here.

"Your Majesties." I managed to keep my voice polite and even, though I merely inclined my head instead of bowing. They may have been a king and queen, but I wasn't in their country and they had given their daughter to a monster. I wasn't about to give them any more than the slightest courtesy, and only that because of how much I loved Nami.

"Mr. Stirling." King Raj shifted on the step as if he planned to come inside.

Immediately, I folded my arms across my chest, solidifying my presence in the doorway. If he wanted inside, he would have to get by me, and I didn't like his chances. He wasn't a small man, but I was bigger, and younger. And I was pissed.

"Please, let us see our daughter," the queen spoke this time. There was a pleading note in her voice, but I didn't move.

"Reed."

160

Nami spoke up from behind me and I glanced over my shoulder.

"It's okay."

I had my doubts, but they were her parents. As long as they didn't try to take her out of the house by force, they couldn't hurt her by coming in. I knew I didn't have to worry about them talking her into coming back to Tanek, not with Halea still in the kitchen.

I stepped to one side and the queen rushed past me and threw her arms around Nami. I wasn't sure who was more surprised, her or me. Then the king stepped inside and turned towards me, his hand out.

Well, shit.

As I shook his outstretched hand, movement outside caught the corner of my eye. When the king moved to embrace his daughter as well, I looked towards the road. Kai and Tomas were standing at the car. They gave me identical nods and I felt a rush of relief. The fact that they were here meant, I hoped, that they'd gotten Ina to the king and queen, and that Tanek was done.

I closed the door behind me and turned to find Halea in her father's arms and Queen Mara wiping her eyes. Nami looked at me, her own eyes wet and shining. She motioned towards the couch and chairs that Piper had left behind.

"Let's sit."

161

I let them all settle, unsure where I should sit. King Raj took one of the chairs and Halea perched on the arm, grinning from ear to ear. Queen Mara sat on the couch and Nami took the seat in the middle. She looked up at me and smiled, gesturing to the spot next to her. I took it, but didn't touch her. We needed to deal with one issue at a time.

"Kai and Tomas brought a young lady to speak with us," King Raj glanced at Halea, obviously choosing his words carefully. "Ina told us about her own...experiences with Tanek."

Nami's face tightened.

"And then they told us about you." King Raj looked at me, his eyes narrowed. "About how you and Nami met, and the time you spent together."

Oh, fuck me.

I didn't know what the expression on my face was, but I did see the stubborn set to Nami's jaw, the rebellious glint in her eyes. She reached over and took my hand.

"Did they?" Her voice was cool.

"They did," Queen Mara said dryly. "Enough that they knew they could be in serious trouble for their dereliction of duty."

My fingers twitched against Nami's, but she remained calm and collected.

"What else did my bodyguards tell you?"

I caught a flash of something in the king's eyes,

162

something that looked like a combination of admiration and annoyance. It was quickly replaced with something else. Regret.

"The truth about what we had done to you." King Raj stood and crossed over to where we were sitting. To my shock, he went down on his knees in front of Nami. "We were wrong, my child. So wrong." His voice caught on the last word and he grabbed Nami's free hand. "I will never forgive myself for what that..." He uttered a word in their native language that, based on the shocked look on Nami's face, I assumed was suitably appropriate for Tanek. "For what he did to you."

Nami's fingers tightened around mine. Kai and Tomas didn't know the worst of it. I hadn't told them all the things I knew Tanek had done, only that he'd been abusing her. That meant the king and queen didn't know.

"He's in jail," Queen Mara said. She smoothed down Nami's hair. "And he will never hurt you again."

King Raj turned to me, still on his knees. "Thank you, Reed, for saving my daughters when I was too blind to see what was happening."

I didn't know if this was the right time, but I wouldn't go another moment without saying it. If they knew that Nami and I had slept together when we'd first met, and it seemed like they did, they needed to know the whole truth of it. "I love her."

Nami's hand squeezed mine almost to the point of pain. She clearly hadn't expected that, but she didn't look angry at my confession.

"Do you?" Queen Mara's voice was cool, but not cold.

"I do." I made the words firm as I turned to meet the queen's eyes. They were Nami's eyes, almost the exact same shade of blue-green. "And I'll protect her with my life."

"From what we hear, you almost did just that." King Raj stood. "And we won't forget it."

"Neither will I," Nami said softly. Her parents looked at her. "What I want to know is, with all this talk of being sorry coupled with what you owe Reed – have you learned anything?"

The atmosphere immediately changed and I could feel the tension radiating off of all three of them.

"You say you'll never forgive yourself for what happened," she continued. "But that doesn't mean anything to me if you're not willing to change."

"Change?" King Raj's voice was soft.

Nami lifted her chin. "You forced me to marry a man I didn't choose. A man who beat me. Raped me. Repeatedly."

My fingers were nearly numb from how hard she was squeezing my hand.

The queen made a noise, confirming my previous suspicion that they hadn't known about the rapes.

"All because of tradition." Her voice was steady, but I could feel her body shaking against mine. "You never once asked what I wanted. Never asked my opinion on anything." She looked at her mother and then at her father. They both flinched at the look in her eyes. "And this is what happened because of it."

"What do you want?" Queen Mara asked. "What can we do?"

"Annul my marriage."

Okay, that one took me off guard, and judging by the look on her parents' faces, they hadn't been expecting it either though I wasn't sure why I was surprised. Of course she wouldn't want to stay married to Tanek. I just hadn't realized that her parents had any power to control that.

"Annul the marriage," Nami repeated. "And let me choose. Choose my own life."

"And if we do," King Raj said slowly. "If we let you choose, what will your choice be?"

"I will be Queen," Nami said. "I accept that responsibility." She took a deep breath and then added, "And I choose him."

My heart gave an unsteady thump.

King Raj looked at me, a stern expression on his face, and then turned to his wife. She nodded and they both looked at Nami.

"Agreed," King Raj said. "Let us discuss where we go from here."

Chapter 18

Nami

I put my hands on the edge of the sink and bowed my head. The bathroom was full of steam, my skin still glistening. The hot water had done a great job of easing the knots in my back and shoulders, but my whole body was still tense. The past few days, hell, the past few weeks, hadn't been easy, but today had been what Americans would have called a roller coaster of emotions.

Joy at seeing my parents. Horror and humiliation when they said Kai and Tomas had told them about what Tanek had done, about the truth behind mine and Reed's relationship. The surge of love hearing Reed say that he loved me and he'd protect me. A mix of feelings so complex that I couldn't explain them or sort them as my parents asked for my forgiveness, acknowledged that they owed Reed. And then surprise at my own boldness when I challenged them.

They would annul my marriage, had promised to make the necessary calls that very afternoon. By the time we returned to Saja tomorrow, I would be free of my vows. Free to publicly choose Reed.

I swallowed hard. If he still wanted me.

I pulled the towel off of my head and let the wet curls tumble over my bare shoulders. I hung it up on the door hook and turned back to the sink. I had another towel wrapped around me and I took that off now. I looked down at my body. The bruises were nearly gone. I'd never bruised easily and they'd always healed quickly. It wasn't them I was looking at though.

I was looking for other changes.

"Nami?" Reed knocked on the door. "Are you okay?"

"Fine," I said. "I'll be out in a moment."

I pulled the towel back around me again, looked one more time at the little piece of white plastic, then threw it in the trash. After a moment's consideration, I covered it with a bit of toilet paper even though there were only two of us in the apartment at the moment. Halea might have gone back to the hotel with my parents, but I didn't want him finding out that way either.

No, he deserved to hear it from me.

I walked out of the bathroom and across the hall to the bedroom Reed and I had been using. The fact that my parents had left the two of us here, knowing we were sleeping together, was their way of saying I could make my own decisions. That they'd accepted my choice. In a few minutes, I'd know if my choice would accept me. I knew he loved me, that he was willing to go to jail for me, but this was different. For some men, this would break them.

"Are you sure you're okay?" Reed came towards me as I stepped into the room. He took my hand, an expression of concern on his face. "You look like you're feeling sick."

I shook my head even though he was partially right. I did feel like I was going to throw up, but this time I knew it really was from nerves. The other times I'd told myself it was nerves, I knew now I'd been lying to myself. I'd probably known it then, but so much had been going on, I hadn't wanted to think about it. And I certainly hadn't wanted to think about the implications.

"I have something I need to tell you." For the first time today, my voice shook.

"Nami, sweetheart, what's wrong?" He put his hand on the side of my face. "You're scaring me, love."

"I—" Words failed me and I ducked my head.

"You can tell me anything." He cupped my chin, raising my head so that I was looking at him. I could see the fear mingling with concern. "Even if it's that you changed your mind about me."

I shook my head, tears burning in my eyes. "I haven't. I love you and I want you. I wish I would have chosen you from the beginning."

"I wish that too," he said, brushing his thumb across the corner of my eye. "If only to have spared you from the pain of what happened."

"It's not just that." I took a breath and wished I had the courage to take a step back, the strength to say this without needing his touch.

"Please, just tell me."

It was the desperation in his voice that did it.

"I'm pregnant."

I waited, but other than a slightly stunned look on Reed's face, there was no reaction. No cursing. No pushing me away. Neither was there joy or excitement. I hadn't expected that though. Shock had been the best I'd hoped for. After all, I hadn't thought anything of it when Reed and I had made love those few times since he'd come for me, hadn't thought to tell him that we needed to use a condom.

I was able to move away now and his hands fell at his sides.

"There's more," I forced myself to say it. "I haven't taken my birth control since we were in Venice. So when we've...and when Tanek..." Bile rose in my throat and I choked it down. The words that came out next were just as bitter on my tongue. "I don't know who the father is."

Tears streamed down my cheeks and I dropped my head, unable to look at Reed, to see whatever expression was on his face. Rejection. Disgust. Even pity.

Then his arms were around me, pulling me against his bare chest. He held me tight, making soothing noises that had no words. His skin was hot and I welcomed the heat, my own body cold from my confession.

"Do you know what I know?" Reed's voice was soft, but there was no hesitation, no wavering. "I know that it doesn't matter whose DNA that child has, I am its father."

I caught my breath and looked up at him, not daring to hope that I was understanding him correctly.

"I don't care if this is too fast or if people think I'm crazy." His expression was fierce. "I love you, Namisa Carrmoni, and if you'll have me, I want to marry you."

I wanted to say yes so badly, but I couldn't. Not when I knew why he was saying it. Maybe we would get there in some distant future, but I didn't want it to come like this.

"I won't let you do that," I said.

"Won't let me?" he asked.

"I won't have you marrying me just because I'm

pregnant."

He shook his head and released me, taking a step back. "If you don't want to marry me, Nami, all you have to do is say it. I would never force the issue." He looked away. "I just thought, that since you said you wanted me, that you chose me..."

"I do," I said. "And I did choose you."

"Then why won't you marry me?"

The question was so sad that my heart broke. "I do want to marry you. I just don't want it to be because..."

I didn't get to finish because Reed's mouth was covering mine, swallowing my protests. The towel fell to the floor and his hands were on me, running down my back to my ass and back up again, leaving burning trails of fire along my skin. His tongue slid between my lips, curling around mine and drawing it into his mouth. I moaned, everything else forgotten but the feel of his chest under my hands, the way his teeth were scraping against my bottom lip.

I made a muffled squeak as he picked me up and felt him smile. He lowered me to the bed, finally releasing my mouth so that he could kiss his way down my neck. His lips danced across my skin, up my breasts, pausing to circle my nipple with his tongue, then moving to the other one. I expected him to either return to my mouth or move lower to

172

the aching place between my legs. Instead, he stopped at my stomach, placing a kiss just above my bellybutton. He ran his fingers across my skin, his expression thoughtful as he looked at my stomach.

"Is that really the only reason?" he asked softly, not looking up at me. "You don't want me to feel obligated?"

"Yes." I reached down and ran my fingers through his hair.

He looked up at me, his eyes deep pools of black. "I love you, Nami. And that has nothing to do with...this." He spread his hand across my stomach. "I want to marry you." He smiled softly, his fingers moving slowly over my still-flat belly. "Not in spite of, or because of." He leaned forward and kissed my stomach again. "I want to have a family with you. It doesn't matter to me that things are moving faster than I'd thought they would. It's what I want because it's you." He looked at me again. "What do you want, Nami?"

I gave him the truth. "You." I cupped his chin, using it to pull him back up my body.

"Then marry me," he whispered against my mouth.

"Yes." I pulled his head down so that our lips crashed together.

His hands moved down my body as we kissed and then I felt his cock between my legs, pushing against me. He pulled his mouth away long enough for our eyes to meet and me to nod my consent. Then he was sliding inside me and the world was reduced to just the two of us. Our bodies moving together, hips rising and falling in perfect sync. The pleasure was building fast inside me, driving me towards the inevitable explosion. And when it happened, Reed was there with me, calling out my name.

This was what I wanted. Not only the sex, but the completeness that came with joining with someone who knew me, understood me on some level that no one else did. Reed wasn't just a great lover, he was my other half. He made me a better woman. He was the one I wanted to spend the rest of my life with, the man I wanted to be the father of my children, no matter what biology said.

I didn't know how the people of Saja would react to any of this, but for the first time in my life, that wasn't what mattered. For the first time, I was going to have something I wanted.

Chapter 19

Reed

We left Philadelphia Friday morning and Nami didn't ask why I hadn't gone to see my parents before we left. I'd been a little worried that she would think I didn't want them to know about the engagement or the baby, but she seemed to understand that I wasn't ashamed of her but rather didn't want to deal with all of the shit that would inevitably follow a visit to my parents.

I did, however, take her with me into the bank where I'd kept a small safe deposit box with a few things I didn't want to take with me as I traveled. One of those things was my grandmother's engagement ring. It hadn't been expensive enough for Britni, but I knew Nami didn't care about that. The moment she saw the ring, her face lit up and she held out her hand.

Judging from the expression on her parents' faces when we met them at the airport, the ring came as no surprise. Halea, however, was thrilled. We took a private plane back to Italy and she spent at least half of it talking to Nami about what the wedding would be like. The queen joined in, assuring Nami that before the plane landed in Saja, the marriage to Tanek would be annulled. The only question was how long we wanted to wait before we held the wedding.

I felt Nami's eyes on me when her mother asked the question again. I looked up from where I'd been on my phone, reading all the emails I'd ignored over the past week. My parents were responsible for at least half of them, some business, some personal. I supposed they figured that at least this way there was a chance they'd get to have their say. I put all that aside though. My parents could wait.

"Whatever you want," I said quietly. I understood what she was asking and I would let it be her decision. If we married quickly, then announced the pregnancy in six weeks or so, we might be able to pass off the child as having been legitimately conceived on our wedding night, just born early.

I didn't know what Saja annulments required, but there was a chance that they were the same as American annulments which, as far as I knew, required a marriage not be consummated. In my mind, consummation meant consent, but I didn't know about the laws in Saja. If an announcement of the marriage being annulled meant that the people of Saja believed Nami and Tanek hadn't slept together, then they would believe that the child was mine.

It was mine, I thought fiercely. Nami was mine. My family.

"We would like to marry as soon as possible," Nami said. "There is no need for something lavish. As we all know, that does not guarantee a happy marriage."

"We will be arriving late and we will need to adjust to the time change," King Raj said. "But if you wish, we could conduct the ceremony tomorrow." He looked at me. "Do you have any specific religious affiliations that you wish us to include?"

I was surprised by the question. While the king and queen were honoring their word about letting Nami choose what she wanted to do with her life, I'd expected them to tolerate me, especially since they knew little about me save that I'd had sex with their daughter before she'd been married to Tanek. Well, that and the whole rescuing thing, which I sincerely hoped made them think better of me than the rest.

"My family attended church back in Philadelphia, but it was a social thing. They go because it's expected of them. I'm happy to follow whatever customs Saja follows." I smiled at Nami. "Nami is my family now."

I saw her hand go to her stomach and wondered at how quickly the gesture became natural.

"And speaking of family," she said.

I was a bit surprised she was going to tell her parents and Halea, but I'd meant what I'd said. I would support what she wanted.

"I'm pregnant."

Queen Mara's mouth tightened for a moment, her eyes going from Nami to me and back again.

"Who is...?" The king was obviously thinking the same thing, but couldn't quite bring himself to ask it.

Nami's eyes met mine and I knew she'd let me decide this one. It wasn't even a consideration. "I am."

"For certain?" King Raj gave me a cynical look.

"Yes." I stood and walked over to Nami. I reached down and took her left hand, raising it to kiss her ring. "They're both mine." Her eyes shown and she tilted her head up so I could kiss her lips. Mindful of the eyes on me, I kept the kiss chaste and brief. Still, it sent electricity through me and I had to remind myself that I only had to wait until tonight, tomorrow night at the latest, and I could indulge in a more thorough kiss. That and more. I ran the back of my hand down the side of her face. I'd never get enough of her.

"Tomorrow, then," Queen Mara said. "We have

plenty of time on the journey home to plan a wedding."

"And a nursery." Halea was beaming. "I wonder if it is a boy or a girl."

I left the sisters to talk with their mother and went to get a drink for myself and the king. I had a feeling, with all of the wedding and baby talk, King Raj and I were going to need a drink. Him, because of the events of the past couple days. Me, not because of my impending marriage or fatherhood. I wasn't nervous about either one, at least not about my choices. No, I was going to do something else that was freaking me out.

I was going to send an email to my parents with an invitation to my wedding and an offer to pay for a private plane.

By Saturday afternoon, I still hadn't heard from my parents and I put it all aside as I made my way out of the guest chamber where I'd slept last night. Alone, unfortunately, but understandably. Very little about this wedding would be traditional, but I could at least stay away from Nami until the ceremony. A ceremony where I would have no one at my side. My parents had made their decision and my conscience was clean. I'd leave Philadelphia and my family in the past. Today was about moving forward. New life. New home. New family.

As soon as I walked into the garden – the little

one that Nami loved so much, not the big one – I saw two familiar faces.

"Piper! Julien!" I stared at my friends as they hurried over.

"Nami called me when you guys landed in Italy," Piper said, pulling me into a quick hug. "She wanted you to have someone here to stand with you." When she stepped back to Julien's side, her smile faltered. "Unless you think this is too weird."

"No." I shook my head and gave them both smiles. "It's definitely good to see some friendly faces."

"Yeah, those two don't exactly look like the friendly type." Julien gestured over my shoulder.

I glanced back and laughed. Kai and Tomas were standing on either side of the entrance, looking very much like the menacing former linebackers I'd once thought they were. "Actually, they're good guys. Threatened to kick my ass a time or two...and one of them once said he'd castrate me if I got near Nami again, but we've worked out our differences."

Julien glanced down at Piper, a smile playing on his lips. They had one of those moments of silent communication that I understood now.

"It's good to see you happy, Reed," Piper said sincerely. "Ever since...well, it's all I wished for you."

"I know," I smiled at her. "I am happy, and I owe you two quite a bit for that."

"Not at all," Julien said. He held out his hand. "It's what friends do."

"Yes," I agreed as I shook his hand. "It is."

The music changed as the string quartet saw the king and queen ready to enter. Piper and Julien hurried off to stand with a handful of other spectators I didn't know but assumed I'd be meeting later on. I took a step backwards until I was off the path and gave a slight bow as my soon to be in-laws walked past.

Halea followed them, dressed in a simple pale blue dress that made me realize that Kai and Tomas were going to have their hands full soon, keeping guys away from her. Halea and the queen moved until they were across from the other members of the audience and the king stood at the top of the path. He looked at me and I took a deep breath. It was my turn.

I walked up the path and took my place to the right, turning as the music changed again. It wasn't a traditional American wedding march, but that didn't matter. The moment I saw Nami walk between Kai and Tomas, nothing else mattered. The heat, the fact that my parents hadn't even acknowledged my invitation, not knowing how this country would accept me. Right now, I didn't care about anything except the beautiful woman walking towards me.

Her dress matched Halea's, a shimmering blue that contrasted with her darker skin and made her eyes glow even more brightly. She wasn't far enough along to be showing, but I found myself looking anyway. Beneath the soft curves of her body was a child. Our child. My heart constricted painfully and I wondered how my body could handle everything I was feeling. It was strange, I thought, how I'd once thought I'd loved Piper. What I'd felt for her was so small compared to what I felt for Nami, and even though it seemed impossible, I found myself loving Nami more with each passing day.

I barely heard King Raj speaking as Nami took her place at my side. As I'd been instructed, I held out my arm and she placed hers so that our hands were on top of each other. We'd agreed for a less formal ceremony, cutting out a lot of what the king had said at the prior ceremony, so it was only a short time later that I found myself repeating a vow to love and honor Namisa Carrmoni as my wife and my queen. Her voice was steadier than mine when she said her own vow, but I could see the tears glistening in her eyes as I slid her wedding band onto her finger. It was a beautiful piece of workmanship, surprisingly complementary to my grandmother's ring. Simple white gold, it had been handed down through the generations, though Tanek had refused to use it in place of his own mother's rings. I was glad he hadn't. It meant so much to Nami and there were no negative memories associated with it. While I knew both of us would never forget what had happened, neither of us wanted the memories to haunt us, taint what we had. Fittingly, the inscription on the inside of the band, roughly translated, said 'Your past is gone. We are the future'.

And then I was instructed to kiss my bride. I looked down at her and gently took her face between my hands. It didn't matter that her parents and sister were here, that people were watching. This moment was about her and me, a promise that this was it. Neither of us were going to run away. No matter what the future held, we would stand together.

I let her see all of that in my eyes and then I bent my head forward to, for the first time, kiss my wife.

nursery was dim, but I could make out the expression on her face. She was worried I'd be angry at her.

"I had the paternity test done. I had to know."

I captured her always wayward curl. "I don't need a test to tell me that she's mine. Biology doesn't determine family."

Nami nodded. "I know." She reached up and ran her finger along my bottom lip. "And I think we should start trying to give her a brother soon." Her eyes were the deep blue-green of the ocean. "A full-blooded brother who looks exactly like her father."

"Nami?" I made it a question.

She nodded, a smile breaking across her face as she pushed herself up on her toes so she could press her mouth against mine. It was a hard kiss, a fierce one. "After all," she continued. "Her father is the most handsome man in the world."

I wrapped my arms around her and lifted her so that we were face to face. "Do you mean it?"

"Yes." She rested her forehead against mine. "The test..."

"Not that," I interrupted. "About wanting to try for another baby already?"

She laughed, a soft sound so as not to wake our daughter. "It probably won't happen right away since I'm still breast-feeding her, but yes."

"We should still probably get started." I shifted

my grip on her, moving my hands down to grab her ass. She wrapped her legs around my waist and I walked her back to the wall.

"Here?" She gasped as I kissed her neck.

"Yes," I said. "Here. Now."

I tugged on the belt of her robe, making a sound low in my throat as the silk fell away to reveal her amazing body. She'd worried, I knew, that I wouldn't find her attractive after Angelique was born, that the way her body had changed would repulse me. I'd spent an entire night focused on worshipping every inch of her so that she would never feel that doubt again.

"What if she wakes up?" Nami asked, then moaned as I lowered my head to flick my tongue across her nipple. Her breasts were even more sensitive and responsive than they had been before. I'd actually made her come once just from paying attention to them. Turns out I love the way she tastes.

"I guess you need to be quiet then." I grinned at her as I reached between us and pushed down the shorts I'd been planning on wearing to bed. Now I was thinking that naked might be the way to go.

I was already hard, my body begging me to bury myself inside her, but I waited. I twisted my fingers, ignoring the awkward angle, and slid my hand between her legs. She moaned again, biting her

188

bottom lip to muffle the sound. She was already wet when I slipped a finger inside her. So wet and tight.

"*Please, my love.*" She dug her nails into the back of my neck.

I positioned myself and grabbed her hip, holding her as I slid home. We groaned in unison, eyes closing as we came together. With all of the responsibilities that came with being the heir to the crown, as well as refusing to yield to the common practice of allowing a wet nurse and nanny take primary care of our daughter, time alone was precious. And far too infrequent.

She clung to me as I moved in deep, even strokes that filled her completely. Her full breasts pressed against my chest and she wrapped her arms more tightly around my neck, her breath hot against my skin as she whispered endearments and encouragements in two languages.

I could feel the tension coiling in my stomach and fought against it. I needed her to come first. I swore quietly as her teeth scraped over my throat, then bit down. The pull of her mouth as she sucked on my skin made my muscles tremble and I knew I wouldn't last much longer.

"*Come, baby. Please,*" I begged her, surprised that I could even remember the words.

She shuddered and I rolled my hips, pressing harder against her clit. Her teeth clamped down

haven't gotten much of that either lately."

I bent my head and covered her mouth with mine. The kiss was deep and thorough, leaving us both gasping for air by the time I raised my head.

"You win," she said. "More of that, then sleep."

"Deal."

As we stood, I glanced over at the cradle one more time. My daughter. My angel. I smiled. Maybe she did look a little like me after all. Nami squeezed my hand and I let her pull me through the adjoining door and into our bedroom. Even as the door closed behind us, I took her into my arms and walked us over to our bed. I planned on taking my time now. If Nami had her way, we'd have half a dozen kids in as many years and who knew how many opportunities we'd have for leisurely love-making.

I wouldn't have it any other way.

THE END

Acknowledgement

First, I would like to thank all of my readers. Without you, my books would not exist. I truly appreciate each and every one of you.

A big "thanks" goes out to all my Facebook fans, street team, beta readers, and advanced reviewers. You are a HUGE part of the success of my series.

I have to thank my PA, Shannon Hunt. Without you my life would be a complete and utter mess. Also a big thank you goes out to my editor Lynette and my wonderful cover designer, Sinisa. You make my ideas and writing look so good.

About The Author

M. S. Parker is a USA Today Bestselling author and the author of the Erotic Romance series, Club Privè and Chasing Perfection.

Living in Southern California, she enjoys sitting by the pool with her laptop writing on her next spicy romance.

Growing up all she wanted to be was a dancer, actor or author. So far only the latter has come true but M. S. Parker hasn't retired her dancing shoes just yet. She is still waiting for the call for her to appear on Dancing With The Stars.

When M. S. isn't writing, she can usually be found reading– oops, scratch that! She is always writing. ☺

Printed in Great Britain
by Amazon

30191203R10116